Damn the Confed!

He took a deep breath, as he exhaled both air and anger. Somebody had to do something. Somebody had to stop the Confed, had to make it release its steel grip, had to end its casual death-dealing.

He laughed into the rain. Who? Him? By himself? But even the largest army was made up of single units. And if a man were careful . . . If he were clever and skilled . . .

Yes! He'd trained, he'd studied. Now it was time to *act*.

He went looking for the man with the strange, silent weapons. . . .

Ace Books by Steve Perry

The Matador Series

THE MAN WHO NEVER MISSED
MATADORA
THE MACHIAVELLI INTERFACE
THE ALBINO KNIFE
BLACK STEEL

THE 97TH STEP
THE OMEGA CAGE (written with Michael Reaves)

STEVE PERRY
THE MAN WHO NEVER MISSED

ACE BOOKS, NEW YORK

THE MAN WHO NEVER MISSED

An Ace Book / published by arrangement with
the author

PRINTING HISTORY
Ace edition / August 1985

ISBN: 0-441-51918-0

Ace Books are published by The Berkley Publishing Group,
200 Madison Avenue, New York, New York 10016.
The name "ACE" and the "A" logo
are trademarks belonging to Charter Communications, Inc.

PRINTED IN THE UNITED STATES OF AMERICA

10 9 8 7 6 5

For Dianne, forever

ACKNOWLEDGMENTS

There are people who helped—if you like the book, you can give them a big part of the credit; if not, it's all my fault for screwing up their perfectly good input.

With that in mind, thanks go:

To Dianne Perry, for an argument over breakfast one morning, in which I had a came-to-realize moment about violence.

To Slick Reaves, for having my best interests at heart—and for old man Kamus.

To Beth Meacham, for her work in selling The Committee and despite her lousy timing after that.

And, finally, to Johann Pachelbel, still on the hit parade after three hundred years. . . .

Strategy is the craft of the warrior.
—MIYAMOTO MUSASHI

*One must therefore be a fox to recognize traps
and a lion to frighten wolves.*
—MACHIAVELLI

The villain is the system.
—PEN

ONE

DEATH CAME FOR him through the trees.

It came in the form of a tactical quad, four people walking the three-and-one, the point followed by the tight concave arc; the optimum number in the safest configuration. It was often said the Confed's military was always training to fight the last war and it was true enough, only there had been enough last wars to give them sand or cold or jungle troops as needed. These four were jungle-trained, they wore class-one shiftsuits with viral/molecular computers able to match backgrounds within a quarter second; they carried .177 Parkers, short and brutal carbines which held five hundred rounds of explosive ammo—one man could cut down a half-meter-thick tree with two waves of his weapon on automatic. The quad carried heat-sensors, com-implants, Doppler gear and personal sidearms; they were the deadliest and best-equipped soldiers the Confed could field and they were good. They moved through the cool rain forest quietly and efficiently, alert for any signs of the Shamba Scum. If something moved, they were going to spike it, hard.

Khadaji felt the fear in himself, the familiar coldness in the pit of his belly, an old and unwelcome tenant. He had learned to live with it, it was necessary, but he was never comfortable when it came to this. He took a deeper breath and pressed his back harder against the rough bark of the sumwin tree. He practiced invisibility. The tree was three meters thick, they couldn't see him, and even without his confounder gear their directional doppler and heat sensors wouldn't read through that much solid wood. He listened as they moved past him. The soft ferns brushed against the shiftsuits of the quad; the humus of a thousand years made yet softer sounds under their slippers as they walked, but Khadaji knew exactly where they were when he stepped away from his tree.

He was behind them, a tall figure in plain tan orthoskins with spetsdöds molded to the backs of both hands. He held his breath for steadiness and brought his arms up, as might a man lifting a small child. He hyperextended the index fingers of both hands and each of the spetsdöds fired once, a polite cough. Two hits, sounding like knuckles on wood as they pierced the too-light armor.

They were fast, the last two. The bacterially-augmented reflexes had been well-trained, but in this case, the instruction was wrong. Instead of dropping flat, the point and left rear spun, carbines cleared for killing.

Khadaji fired both spetsdöds again. The flechettes hit the soldiers halfway through their turns, on the sides instead of the backs. The point managed to trigger off a few rounds before he crumpled. The sound of the .177 was very loud in the thick forest. The smell of the electro-chemical explosive tainted the air with an acrid tang.

The four soldiers were knotted into odd angles amid the ferns and spider plants, voluntary muscles clenched in the frozen lock which gave the ion/molecular/chemical flechette of the spetsdöd its name: Spasm. They wouldn't die, but it would take six months of treatment to bring them back to normal. Six months of extensive physical and psychotherapy for each victim of the spetsdöd's sting, expensive, time-consuming, draining. Spetsdöds were good weapons for guerrillas—a dead man cost the enemy little, but a Spasm-ed soldier was a lot of work; with proper treatment, they never died and they did cost.

Khadaji turned to leave. One of the quad might have triggered his com and, if so, a flier would already be on its way. As he started to move, he glanced back at the soldiers. One of them had a stain on his leg. It was hard to see because of the shiftsuit, which matched the color of the ground on which the downed man lay, but it looked like blood.

He moved closer. Yes. Apparently the point's desperation blast had wounded one of his own. Damn!

Khadaji hurried to the man. No, correction, it was a woman, not that it mattered. She was hit, there was a crater the size of his fist in her thigh and she would bleed to death in a few minutes.

For a moment, Khadaji thought about it. He hadn't killed any of them, so far, and this one wouldn't be on his karma, he hadn't shot her. A flier might be coming.

He shook his head. No. He had to take the long view.

He found her medical kit and jerked it from her belt. He opened the plastic case and found the pressure patch. Triggering the unit, he slapped it over the pumping hole in her leg. The patch whined and sealed around the edges. Inside, the pressure went up as the rudimentary brain of the medical sealer clamped arteries and veins and shuttled the flow of blood. If a flier was coming, she'd be all right. Once he got away from the woods, he would call and report the downed quad anyway, so there was no real danger. There were no predators on Greaves and the most dangerous thing which could happen to the quad was that they might get rained on.

Khadaji rose from his crouch and looked at the quad a final time before he loped off into the woods. He managed a grin against the drop of adrenaline which left him feeling drained and tired. The Shamba Scum had struck again— according to the official dispatches, their number was now estimated at between six and eight hundred. His smile increased. If the quad he'd just downed had been faster, the Shamba Scum would have been eliminated—all of them. For Emile Antoon Khadaji *was* the resistance on Greaves, all by himself.

It was six klicks to his next station. He jogged the whole way, alert for any sounds of more troops or fliers. It was quiet. The earthy smell of the mushrooms and molds was heavy—brought out by the rain last night—and the ground was squishy underfoot.

This part of it was hard, too. Aside from the means, the logistics were becoming more difficult all the time. In the early days, it had been easy. The Confed's machine came to rest on Greaves as it had a dozen other peaceful worlds almost without incident. There were no armies on the world, no underground brewing among the agros and craftspeople who made up most of the planet's population. Oh, there had been a few students handing out agitprop, but nothing of any consequence—until ten or twenty troops a day began dropping with Spasm poisoning. A single message, coded mysteriously into the Garrison Commander's computer, claimed responsibility in the name of the Shamba Freedom Forces—quickly shortened to Shamba Scum by the troops-of-the-line.

Khadaji grinned as he ran along the thin path through the forest. That had been a nice touch, he'd thought, naming the "Freedom Forces" after Lord Thomas Reserve Shamba, the twenty-second century war hero. It was a joke only Khadaji could appreciate, though. It came from Shamba's answer to a surrender call by Confed forces who outnumbered him fifty-to-one at the Battle of Mwanamamke in the Bibi Arusi System:

To the Commander, Confederation Jumptroopers:
Sir:
Fuck you.
We stand until the last man falls.

When the first man fell in the current insurgency, it would *be* the last man.

Khadaji slowed to a walk when he was a kilometer from the patrol line. He checked his confounder, to make sure it was operating, bent and stretched his legs and back, and took several deep breaths. There were three men on the line in this sector, virgins as near as he could tell. He could have taken them on the way out, but that might have made it tough to get back into the city. The Confed military mind was rigid and not particularly bright, but neither was it completely stupid. The replacements for these three wouldn't be fresh meat, they'd be vets, more interested in staying ambulatory than proving how well they'd absorbed their training.

The first soldier was so easy it made Khadaji sad. He walked to within five meters without being noticed. The boy—he could have been no older than twenty-two or three—stood in the shade of a small fir tree. It was not particularly warm, but he wore class two body gear, and it didn't take much to heat up the inside of that to sweatpoint. The boy had shifted his goggles up and his tight hood back, exposing his face and head to the cooler air. If Khadaji had been an uprank, the boy would have been in trouble.

"Excuse me, which way is Hartman Street?"

The boy turned, surprised. He started to swing the Parker

up, but stopped. What he saw was a tall man in orthoskins, palms supinated, looking harmless.

"Jeet, dork, don't slip up on a man like that!" He seemed to relax a little, seeing that Khadaji was unarmed and smiling.

The Shamba Scum shrugged, raised his left hand slightly, and stiffened his index finger. "Sorry," he said.

The little dart hit the boy high on the forehead and snapped his face upward; the Spasm hit him on the way down and he was in the lock before he touched the ground. The strongest muscles determined the shape of the knot; this one had strong quads and triceps—his arms and legs stuck out.

Khadaji shook his head. There was no joy in this. The boy would be able to tell all about the man who shot him— in six months, if he were lucky. Meanwhile, he would spend an uncomfortable time thinking about his actions on this day. Spasm froze the muscles but neither the memory nor the mind which drove it. He wouldn't be able to call out, but he would remember how stupid he had been. A harsh punishment for a boy, but it was necessary. All of it was necessary, for reasons this soldier couldn't begin to understand, even if Khadaji had hours to explain it to him.

Unlike the first, the second man wore his armor—and class two would stop a spetsdöd's dart—but the armor wasn't perfect. Gloves and hoods were designed to overlap but the material had to be thin in places for a man to move; knees and elbows and shoulders had to bend or rotate. When the soldier stretched, after two minutes, Khadaji fired. The flechette entered the thin fold behind the man's left knee, a line only a few millimeters wide. It was a difficult shot, but an expert with a spetsdöd could cut a dragonfly in half in mid-air—and hit both pieces as they fell. Point-shooting had been brought to a peak higher than craft, if not art, with the invention of the spetsdöd: the word itself meant "point death."

The brush came alive with the canvas-rip sound of a Parker carbine on full automatic; bushes and trees blew apart, explosive shells chopped them down from waist-level. Khadaji was on the ground and crawling before the first leaves fluttered to the forest floor. The third man had been spooked. Maybe he'd heard or sensed something, maybe one of the others managed to trigger a com. It didn't matter. He was shooting at shades, but he would have called for backup. Khadaji crawled at right angles to the line of fire until he was clear, then stood and ran. Thorns tried to dig into the tough orthoskins, but failed. He dodged trees and larger shrubs, but ran over the small stuff. There was no time for finesse, he had to be a long way from here when help arrived.

He cleared the forest and was among a line of warehouses in the storage district. He stopped. Behind him, half a klick back, the scared soldier was still cutting shrubbery with his weapon.

There were few ways to disguise a spetsdöd on the back of the hand. Khadaji loosened the plastic flesh which connected the two weapons to his body and pulled the flechette guns free. He found a trash bin full of scrap metal and buried the weapons deeply in it. It wouldn't matter if they were found since he had others—the better part of a case of them from the shipment he'd stolen. Twenty spetsdöds and ten thousand rounds of Spasm darts—and that number, ten thousand, was very important.

Although he felt naked without the weapons, Khadaji stepped out onto the street as if he owned it and started toward the Jade Flower. He would have plenty of time to get there and collect another pair of spetsdöds before his last station was due. So far, he'd only taken out five of the Confed's finest, and he needed at least eight more to maintain his schedule. He wanted to average a hundred a week, but it was getting harder all the time. He'd been at it for

almost six months and the first troops would be coming out
of lock pretty soon. When that began to happen, it would
be over. Even if the confed military tried to lid it, word
would eventually get out that only one man's description
kept coming up. They wouldn't believe it, of course, not
at first, but it would plant a seed. They would never admit
that one man could mimic hundreds—military PR would
smash the idea flat, that thousands of trained troops could
be downed by a single assassin. But if they knew, it would
be over fast. They were looking for guerrillas in packs, not
the owner and operator of the Jade Flower, the biggest
recreational chemical pub in the city, a man whose business
depended on the military, as customers and patrons. Soldiers
needed rec-chem almost as much as they needed sex and
the Jade Flower supplied both in abundance. More than a
few of the Sub-Befals spent time there. Khadaji made certain
that upranks got the best whores, male and female, and the
first drink or toke or pop was always on the house to anybody
over line-grade. He was a popular man, Khadaji was.

So, two more stations, six more hits. He sighed. Nearly
six months, and he was getting tired. He didn't waver from
his purpose—that was as clear as ever—but he was tired.
Not much longer. Not many more.

He sighed again, and hurried along the street. A quad
passed him, going the other way. The men all smiled and
nodded at him. He smiled back. He would probably see
them later.

One way or another.

TWO

THE JADE FLOWER was always open. Before the Confed had honored Greaves with its massive squat tactics, the rec-chem pub had been only a small-time operation, serving the locals a narrow spectrum of alcohol and soporifics, minor hallucinogens and mood elevators. Two or three part-time prostitutes took care of anybody interested in buying sex, and the operation was, at best, a break-even proposition. With the coming of the military and its civilian support population, the character of the Jade Flower was bound to change. A greedy and well-prepared man would have made a fortune, but the previous owner was old and tired and not ready to deal with the influx of soldiers, bored spouses and children the Confed bent to the sleepy planet. When Khadaji arrived and waved enough standards under his nose, the old man was glad to sell.

Khadaji looked around the main room of the pub. It was early, not yet 1600, but already the place was crowded.

Even with local zoning regs relaxed, there was usually a line of customers outside, waiting for someone to leave in order to enter. Khadaji always kept a dozen or so places open, for any highly-ranked officers who might be interested in a toke, poke or drink. Anjue, the doorman, had studied the holoproj of every uprank over the level of Lojt and if one showed up, he or she was escorted to the head of the line and inside. Rank, as always, had its privileges. The troops-of-the-line might gripe, but the powers-that-be all smiled at Khadaji when they saw him.

The main room, which was octagonal and dimly-lighted, boasted sixty circular tables with four stools each. The first thing Khadaji had done on buying the pub was to have the stools and tables bolted securely to the floor. He'd had thirty people applying for the job of bouncer and their first test was to see if they could move the furniture. Two men managed to uproot a stool each; one woman set herself and screamed, then tore the top of a table off its mount. And then—well, she was clever. The rest failed. Khadaji had longer bolts installed and hired the two men and woman who'd proved strongest. If a fight broke out, nobody was going to be bashing anybody with his furniture; and before it got too far, Bork, Sleel or Dirisha would be there to stop it. It was difficult to argue with a man holding you a half-meter off the floor, or a woman who could break three ribs with a flat punch. There was very little trouble in the Jade Flower.

"Ho, Emile, how's it hanging?"

Khadaji looked to his right, to see Lojtnant Subru, smoking a flickstick. The man's dark face was almost hidden behind the cloud of purple-black smoke.

"To the left, Subbie, just like always." He grinned. "How's the ratface job?"

Lojtnant Subru shook his head and exhaled a fragrant

blast of flickstick smoke. The smell of hot cashews surrounded Khadaji. "Busy today, Emile. Word is there were several skirmishes within fifty klicks of town."

Khadaji raised an eyebrow and tried to look surprised. "Really? Get any of the Scum?"

The dark soldier nodded. "Body count of fourteen, I heard. They nicked one of ours in a blastfight, but she's okay."

Khadaji didn't have to work very hard to suppress his smile. He'd heard this kind of statistic too many times. "Good for the troops."

"Yeah, we should have the Scum cleaned out pretty soon. Only problem is, I hear IC has upped their estimates of the numbers. Even with the ones we've been cutting down, IC says there are close to a thousand guerrillas in the field now."

Khadaji shook his head. "Where are they coming from?"

"IC would love to know. I hear the Old Man would give his left nut and a kilogram of hauxite to be able to spike the leaders." He took another blast from the flickstick. "You ever do any ratface-time, Emile?"

Khadaji smiled. "Sure. I did my tour sitting planet and pushing disks for a supply unit. Strictly button-thumbing stats, Subbie. Never saw action."

"Yeah? What unit?"

"14-788 Quartermasters, on Tomodachi. Been a few years." The unit was real enough, Khadaji had known men who served in it while he was training, but in fact his own unit had been the 14-433 Jumptroop Plex and he'd seen more action than most of the soldiers on this world. Too much.

The Lojtnant nodded, not really interested. He looked around for a table with an empty stool. "Emile, who's working the sheets tonight? Anybody worth a week's pay?"

"Marj is on, Brin, Roj, Davisito, and . . . let's see, I think Sister Clamp is on at 1800."

"Sister Clamp, huh? I heard she's something else. Expensive, too."

"You can't take it with you, Subbie. Never know but you might get pulled out of that air-conditioned T-plex and put on the line."

"Shee-it, they'll have to be scraping the walls for that. Still, I might get flattened by a ground-effect tank crossing the street. Eighteen, you said?"

"I can put in a word, if you like, maybe get her to give you an uprank discount."

Lojtnant Subru nodded again. "Yeah. Do that, would you? I'd appreciate it."

The soldier wandered off, trailing the smell of cashews.

"Afternoo', Chief."

Khadaji's head pubtender stood there, looking grave.

"Butch. A problem?"

"We runnin' low on mid-range sops. Las' week's delivery was short two gross and we only got half what we need 'til next shipment."

"What do you think, Butch?"

"I think we put a limit on and ration them suckers out."

Khadaji shook his head. "No. Business as usual and when we run out, offer high-range at the same price."

"Jeet, Chief, we lose half a stad every tab!"

"We can afford it, can't we? We want to keep the customers happy."

Butch shook his head. "I don' see how you make an' profit, you keep tryin' to give it away."

"We get by, Butch, we get by."

The pubtender left, looking even more grave than before, and Khadaji began to work his way around the octagon, smiling at the customers, listening and watching as he moved.

"—holes Uplevels wouldn't know a Scum if it peed on—"

"—said she's more fucking *sensitive* than I am—"

"—Jammy's still knotted in the stretch ward—"

"—kid's nine T.S. but sharp, lemme tell you—"

"—couldn't pull it out of her if you wanted to—"

"—the Old Man himself said it, so I hear—"

The flow of conversation was full of the things which have always been important to soldiers: love, hate, sex, money, family, Uplevels' stupidity, the campaign. Khadaji knew the talk. He'd only been nineteen when conscripted for his seven and he'd done six years with men and women like these. Most of them were young, but the military had a way of making you grow up quickly. He was thirty-nine T.S. now, he could have fathered most of the soldiers in the octagon. He felt a lot older than that sometimes, an old man among children.

"—your ass! Get up, elbow-sucker!"

Khadaji froze for an instant, then turned. Two troopers were standing next to a table six meters away, squared off in military oppugnate stances, each waiting for the other to make the first stupid move—which both had already done by standing to fight in the Jade Flower. Khadaji wondered who was on this shift—ah. As he watched, Dirisha moved smoothly through the crowded pub toward the two soldiers. Dirisha was a big woman, close to Khadaji's own 183 cm and eighty-two kilos, but she didn't look it because she was so well balanced. She had short, dark hair, a winning smile when she was happy—like now—and expert rankings in three class one martial arts. She was about twenty-eight T.S. and in a one-on-one, could probably take either Bork or Sleel, the other two bouncers.

Dirisha reached the two men and slid between them, her back to the larger one. Khadaji strolled closer.

"Fighting's not too bright," she said. "I mean, make a list: fucking, soak-toke, good wine or cold simshi and where does getting your face smashed fit in?"

The soldier she was talking to was about eye-level with Dirisha and he was obviously angry. He wasn't going to let go of his rage that easily. "Yeah? Well, I don't think dick-nose over there can smash anything!"

Dirisha's voice got very quiet, and she smiled, her teeth bright against her dark chocolate skin. People strained to hear her. "I wasn't talking about *him* hurting you, Deuce, I'm talking about *me*. You can sit and smoke your smoke or you can walk, but you can't fight in here." Her voice was even and there wasn't a gram of bluff in it.

The soldier seemed to wilt a little.

Khadaji smiled. Dirisha could take the soldier without having to suck a deep breath and the man was perceptive enough to pick up on it, even if he'd never seen her in action. If he had, he would have sat as soon as she approached. He had to get one last shot in, though.

"What about him?" He pointed at the man behind Dirisha.

She didn't bother to turn and look at the second soldier. "He's got the same options you do, Deuce. So what say you just have a seat and work this out like preachlegals." It was not a request.

The tension seemed to drain away suddenly. The larger man behind Dirisha sat on his stool and reached for his mug of splash. The soldier facing Dirisha wiped at the back of his uniform collar with one hand and nodded. "Okay. We don't want any trouble with the Flower, we can work it out later, maybe."

Dirisha's smile broadened. "Good thinking, Deuce. Tell you what, the house buys the next round for this table, tell the server Dirisha okays it."

She turned and walked away quickly, in Khadaji's direction. He smiled at her and she stopped. The pub noises picked back up around them.

"Nice work."

She nodded. "For a second, it could have gone over and I would have had to thump him. You lose points when you have to thump them."

Khadaji nodded. He understood. He had spent much of the fourteen years after Maro studying various fighting disciplines and that had been a point in most of them: to have to use physical technique was a failure of sorts. An expert should be able to project enough *ki* so that a potential opponent would stop hostility. A *real* expert could defuse almost any fight situation simply by *being* there.

"Ever give any thought to your future, Dirisha?"

She shrugged. "I take it as it comes."

He thought about it for a few seconds. It was no riskier than a lot of other things he'd done. He said, "You ever hear of Renault?"

"Backwater world in the Shin System," she said. "I don't know much about it."

"It would be a good place to be in three or four years," Khadaji said, looking past her around the octagon. "Somebody there might make you an offer you'd find interesting."

The big woman looked at him carefully. "What kind of an offer?"

He shrugged. "It might not happen. A lot of things could get in the way. Let's just say if situations go as designed, Renault could be a place for you to stretch yourself a little."

"Um. Any particular place on Renault?"

"There's a small coastal town, Simplex-by-the-Sea."

She didn't say anything for a moment. Then, "But how could I leave you, Emile? You need me here."

He smiled, recognizing the fugue in her statement. "I expect to be out of the rec-chem business pretty soon."

"And on Renault?"

He sighed. "No. You won't see Emile Khadaji on Renault."

She considered that, and apparently decided not to ask anything more. "I'd better get back to work," she said.

"Good idea. I need to check with Anjue and see how the crowd is building. Later."

He watched her move away. She walked with a smooth, rolling motion that bespoke her years of training and excellent physical conditioning. He didn't really know Dirisha; she kept to herself, spent a lot of time working out in one of the local dojos, and had no lovers, male or female, that he knew of. But there was a strength in her beyond the physical, an essence of something deeper. She could be a piece of it, he felt.

He walked to the main entrance of the pub, where Anjue and his three assistants were working the line.

"Anjue. How is it going?"

"Ah, Emile, slow. I have only forty on my flat-screen, and three upranks have called on the com to say they are coming at seventeen." He waved his hands in that typical gesture used by natives of Spandle—a kind of outward loop with each wrist. "The early darkness means a change in guard duty, so fewer troops are free and the eagle doesn't fly for three days, so some are unlined, what can I say?"

"Not to worry, Anjue. We get by."

Khadaji left and headed toward his private rooms in the basement. He stopped by the dispensing window for a moment to tell Butch. The man sat behind a three-centimeter-thick sheet of densecrystal set into a solid plastcrete wall. The drug room might be a tempting target for thieves and it was well protected. The doors were thick stainless steel with reaper locks, and nothing short of a vacuum bomb would dent the densecris window. Chem was purchased and delivered through the double drawers under the window.

"I'm going to catch a little sleep, Butch. No calls for an hour or so."

"Copy, Chief." His voice had a metallic ring through the speaker set into the wall over the window. "We'll try to keep the Scum from takin' over while you're nappin'."

"Thanks, Butch, I appreciate that."

THREE ————————————————

KHADAJI'S PRIVATE SPACE was a combination of office and
living quarters. It was furnished simply—a desk and comp
terminal, a few chairs, a foam-pad bed in one room; a
shower, sink and bidet in the second room; a small kitchen
in the third and final room. Simple living quarters—on the
surface. What didn't show was the hidden store box set
under the floor of his desk, nor the tunnel under the refrig-
erator in the kitchen. He had dug the tunnel himself, using
a "borrowed" cutalong he returned before anyone knew it
was missing. It was a short, tight passage, leading from his
kitchen into the housing of his receiving transformer in the
alley behind the Jade Flower. There was just enough room
for a careful man to stand inside the housing, between the
ceramic insulators and high voltage grid of the transformer.
A careful man could come up through the expanded metal
grate over the floor inside the housing and wait until the
alley was clear to leave. A careless man could not, for he

would be dead, fried by the power circuits.

Khadaji checked his chronometer. Almost seventeen.

From the hidden store box, he took a set of black orthoskins, a pair of spetsdöds and ammunition magazines for them, and a skinmask. This was going to be a city operation and even though it was dark, he didn't want to be recognized. He dressed quickly, tabbing the orthoskins on, smoothing the skinmask over his face and ears and allowing the spetsdöds to set on the backs of his hands. It took a few seconds for the artificial flesh backing the weapons to warm and mold to his own skin; once set, the spetsdöds would be almost as much a part of him as his fingers. The weapons would not shift or move until he triggered the release.

There were a lot more efficient weapons, he knew. Hand wands sent a fan-shaped pulse which could take half a dozen people out at a single strobe; explosive rocket or bullet throwers could blow through armor which would stop a spetsdöd's flechette; implosion bombs wiped away steel as if it were butter. But it had to be spetsdöds. The choice had not been a hard one. Spetsdöds were used by the military sometimes, but they were essentially civilian weapons, so that was a necessity. And a Spasm-loaded dart slinger did not kill, that was another point. Finally, a spetsdöd required skill to use properly, more than wands or explosive guns or bombs. A man who went after targets in class two armor with a spetsdöd was either very good or a fool. A miss and he would likely be dead. That part was as important as any of it, the skill needed. If it was going to be built to work, it had to be built right. He'd had years to think about it and the spetsdöd was the right answer. It had taken him more years to become truly expert in the use of the flechette weapon. There were some better, perhaps, but that didn't matter. He was good enough. He had been so far, at least.

The spetsdöds were ready. He found a set of spookeyes and slipped them on, pushed back on his forehead. He took a sublingual tablet and allowed it to dissolve under his tongue. The chemical had a long and complex name, but it was called Reflex by those who used it. It affected nerves, from peripheral to central nervous system, and its effect was simple enough: the drug speeded up reaction time. The effect varied from person to person, but in Khadaji's case, he was able to move faster than a bacteria-augmented soldier-of-the-line, for short periods. There were some nasty draw-backs to Reflex—it required top physical conditioning to handle because it increased catabolism and metabolism and left the user exhausted afterward; it caused nightmares; it was addictive. Khadaji only used it when he was doing a particularly risky gambit. He would pay for it later.

He checked the skinmask in the mirror, took his con-founder from the box and snapped it into place on his belt. He took a deep breath and nodded at his image. There was one last item: a photon flare. He hooked it onto his belt. He was ready.

His shoulders brushed the flexmac lining the walls of the tunnel as he crawled through it. Carefully, he lifted the matched pad covering the tunnel mouth and moved the expanded metal grate inside the transformer station. It was black inside the cover, with only a thin pattern of streetlight showing through the cooling slots next to the radiant fins over his head. He slid the spookeyes down and clicked them on. The place lit up, in that eerie green of multiply-augmented light. He replaced the pad and grate and stood quietly, lis-tening.

The first rush of Reflex vibrated through him, making him feel warm and slightly itchy. He wanted to move, to run and dance and jump—that was the drug singing to him, urging him to use his body, to do something—anything—fast and hard. But he held still, listening. After a moment, he moved to a slot in the door of the unit and peeped through

it into the alley. Empty. No one home. He clicked the spookeyes off.

In a second, he was through the door and out, locking
it with his thumbprint. He scuttled to the shadows next to
the wall of the Jade Flower and flattened himself against
the cool plastcrete. He would stay in the shadows for this
one. He took a deep breath and moved off, feeling the Reflex
dance in his muscles.

The T-plex was brightly lit, a half-dozen big HT lamps
overlapping their pools of daytime around the building. It
was standard Confed architecture, squat and ugly, a prefab
block of expanded hardfoam with carved door and windows.
Right now, whoever was on electronic watch would be getting signals from Khadaji's confounder and—if they were
awake—wondering what the Doppler ghosts were fuzzing
the screen. The confounder was the best the Confed could
produce—it wasn't even issued to these troops it was so
new—and Khadaji had paid a small fortune for it less than
a year ago. It was unlikely the simadam running the scopes
would know what the problem was.

The lights were something else, of course. The quad did
have image intensification equipment equal to his own. With
spookeyes lit, the quad could see an area framed only in
starlight as if it were a bright afternoon. Shorting the lights
out, therefore, should not be to his advantage.

Khadaji grinned. The problem with the military mind
was that it tended to be logical only to a point that satisfied
it, but no further. The way to out-think the military was to
carry its logic one step past.

He hooked a simple timer-and-popper against the un-
shielded transformer and set the delay for twenty seconds.
He scurried back, keeping to the shadows, until he was in
front of the T-plex. The quad was alert and prowling; no

virgins, these—they were crack troopers, all Sub-Lojts chosen for skill to form this special unit. The woman on the other side of the door they guarded—visible through the hard plastic window—was a Sub-Befalhavare, one of ten on planet. She commanded a thousand troopers and was, therefore, a valuable person. The Confed had done one intelligent thing with its military and that had been to clean up the old-style ranks found on most worlds. The organization had been streamlined for ground troops: four troopers made a quad, commanded by a Sub-Lojt; twenty-five quads formed a centplex, with a Lojtnant running the show; ten centplexes overseen by a Sub-Befalhavare made a ten-kay unit; and the commander of ten thousand troopers was a full Befalhavare. That was the size of the unit on Greaves, a ten kay. The next rank was a Systems Marshal, an Over-Befalhavare, then the Supreme Commander of Confederation Ground Forces Himself. Only five ranks between a line trooper and the S.C.

There was a loud pop and the HT lamps began to fade. Khadaji slid his spookeyes down and flicked them on at minimum, but kept his eyes closed. The intensified light of the dying lamps flashed brilliantly at his closed eyes.

He heard one of the quad yell, "Amplifiers on!"

Good. He was counting on their training. These four would be ready for the darkness by the time the last glimmer faded from the lamps.

Khadaji opened his eyes as the light against them dimmed; he adjusted the spookeyes to compensate for the darkness. Green-on-green images came into ghostly focus. An eye-smiting glare poured from the window of the Sub-Befalhavare's office and he looked away from it, concentrating on the soldiers. With full-intensification, spookeyes would amplify available light millions of times; the glow of a flickstick butt would seem a bonfire at close range.

He had been in the shadows with only a little cover. That

would effectively be gone, now that the light was only from the stars and the ambient city glow. He had to move quickly. And the timing had to be right. They all had to see him at the same time.

"Hey!" Khadaji yelled.

They were superb, the members of this quad. They spun as one, bringing their weapons up.

Khadaji marked their positions in that instant; he also triggered the photon flare and tossed it toward them. He turned his head and squeezed his eyes shut tightly; even so, the light from the flare reflected from the walls beat upon his eyes through the lids. There was no time to think about what it did to the eyes of the quad. Khadaji ran at a right angle to his left, as fast as he could sprint.

The quad was blind, but they were firing. A man's voice began yelling orders over the sound of the .177s and their explosive bullets: "Toomie, take the left, Janie, center front! Jason, to the right!"

Khadaji circled before Jason managed to get his carbine out to cover his assigned field of fire and raised both spets-döds. He fired twice, caught Jason and the quad leader with the first two rounds, then fired both his handguns again. He got Janie, but missed Toomie, who was still covering his quadrant with short bursts of the Parker, his back to Khadaji. Before the man could realize his team wasn't shooting, Khadaji snapped off a final round into Toomie's neck. He went down, the Parker silenced.

No time. Khadaji sprinted for the door, tugging the spookeyes from his face as he ran. He didn't slow, only twisted so that he hit the pressed plastic with his left shoulder. The cheap material tore away from its sliding frame in a shower of gray shards and Khadaji dived for the floor as he went through.

The double boom of a smoothbore pistol filled the air and the charge of brass shot sleeted against the wall and through the open doorway. Khadaji rolled up and fired toward the woman standing behind her desk. The dart hit her square on the chest, but she managed to trigger another twin shot of the smoothbore as she went backwards. The gun was pointed at the ceiling and blew a binocular-shaped pattern in the white hardfoam.

The Sub-Befalhavare went into poison contractions; the strength distribution of her muscles causing her to sit back in her chair, her fists drawn up to her shoulders and her face clenched into a snarl. She held onto the smoothbore pistol at an almost classic port-arms position, pointed by her right ear.

It should not have been funny, but it struck Khadaji that way. He laughed, thought about it for a few seconds, and decided to add a touch more. There was a flower arrangement on the woman's desk and he pulled a long-stemmed green rose from the vase and stuck it into the barrel of the smoothbore. One had to keep one's sense of humor, after all. And it could be a clue for a wise man. A green rose— a jade flower. . . . He doubted the Sub-Befalhavare would think it funny, but humor always depended upon one's view-point, whether you were the one who stepped on the banana peel or an observer.

Time to leave. Khadaji sprinted from the office and into the street. Other troops would be coming and he wanted to be back at the Jade Flower by the time somebody started a net working in the city.

He jumped the downed figure of a quad member near the door and started down the street. Another easy station, he thought, as he ran. He shook his head a little. He had to watch that, the feeling of invincibility, the sense of right-ness which made him feel as if he could not fail. That was dangerous, that kind of thinking. Just because he knew who he was and what he was doing, there was no guarantee he'd succeed. Over-confidence had ruined more than one man, especially men with grand plans who let the big vision cloud the details of the smaller workings. The tendency was to feel as if there was some kind of benevolent spirit backing him, the hand of Fate guiding and protecting him because he was its instrument, and that was dangerous. He was fourteen years past his Realization and he still had to fight the sense of superiority it had given him.

He heard voices approaching from a side street and slid to a halt in the shadow of a trash-recycle hopper. A pair of quads ran by, heading back toward the T-plex. Close.

Yes. It could happen at any time. A stray bullet triggered by a falling trooper could do it, a slip while running from pursuers, any one of a hundred things. For nearly six months he'd been careful and lucky.

He ran back toward the Jade Flower. He recognized that his worry meant the time for the end was getting nearer. It gave him a fluttery stomach to think about it, a tingle in the muscles of his buttocks even as he ran.

"Have a nice nap, Chief?"

"I feel much better, Butch. How's business?"

"Goin' pretty good, now. I heard Anjue on the com a few minutes ago, he said when Sister Clamp came in, fifteen troopers joined the line."

Khadaji nodded and strolled into the octagon. The place was at capacity, save for the spaces saved for upranks. He smiled a little to himself. At least one Sub-Befal wouldn't be dropping by tonight.

There was a man drinking splash alone at one of the spare tables. Khadaji walked to the table and nodded down at the man. He was a quad leader, a Sub-Lojt, and he looked familiar, though Khadaji couldn't place him. "Evening," Khadaji said.

The man looked up and nodded, but didn't speak.

"Drinking alone can be depressing. Mind if I join you?"

The Sub-Lojt shrugged. "Sure. Why not? I was just turning over a few bad memories."

A server brought Khadaji a flare full of Möet & Chandon, from his private stock of vintage champagne. He sipped at the pale amber liquid slowly. "Another splash for the Sub-Lojt," Khadaji said.

"Thanks," the man said. He finished his current mug and leaned back. "You know, I was going to flake out when my impress was up, but I went for another tour. Probably the biggest mistake I ever made."

Khadaji nodded slightly, but said nothing.

"I just left the knot ward—one of my quad is in his second month."

"Hit by the Scum," Khadaji said. That's where he'd seen the man's face, obviously. Only, he couldn't remember the particular attack. There had been so many.

"Yeah. It was dark, we didn't see 'em until it was all over. We were lucky, they only got Rudy. I check on him every once in a while."

"You must really hate them," Khadaji said.

The Sub-Lojt shook his head. "You know what the funny thing is? I don't, really. But seeing Rudy reminds me of what it is I do for a living." The man paused to stare at his splash for a moment. "I was remembering a time on Wu," the trooper said. "That's in the Haradali System."

Khadaji nodded again. "I've heard of it."

"Yeah, well, we had to go in and flatten a local insurrect—bunch of malcons somehow managed to get control of a city and were making a lot of noise. A simple operation, by-the-tape, more gunship diplo than anything else. We waved the flag from a battlecruiser and a couple of support ships and sent a few centplexes down to show Confed muscle, you probably know the drill."

"Yes. I know it."

"Well, I went down with my quad and got stuck doing

guard duty on a secured perimeter, no perspiration. Then, some fuzzbrain in the malcons got the idea to try a raid. They sent maybe a hundred against us, armed with sticks and thero-knives and a few chemical-only slug guns."

The Sub-Lojt paused and took a drink of the new mug of splash. "Stupid," he said. "Practically unarmed against a quad, none of us virgins. We cut them down like it was target practice. It was stupid of them, stupid!"

Khadaji sipped his champagne.

"It was not our fault, they'd have wiped us, they could have, we were only doing our jobs. But after it, I went with the medics to check for survivors. We were using .177s with the harrad load, so there weren't many. But there was this . . . girl." He paused and took another swallow of his drink, closing his eyes as he did. "This girl was maybe thirteen and she was lying there with her legs shot off from from the middle of the thighs down. And she looked up at me while the medics were clamping vessels and pumping dorph into her to kill the pain and I swear I never saw such clear green eyes before or since. And she smiled and said, 'It's all right. My father is a soldier.' And then she died. Massive hemo-shock, the medics said."

The Sub-Lojt finished his splash and set the mug down gently. "That was the bad part. As if it was okay for me to shoot her, because I was a soldier like her father." He shook his head. "A system that makes people kill children, it's just not right. If something like that ever comes up again, I don't know if I could shoot. I haven't seen any of the Shamba Scum, but if I saw a bunch of kids coming at me waving sticks, I just don't know what I'd do this time. Can you understand how I might feel like that?"

Khadaji nodded, and stared unseeing at the far wall of the octagon. "Yes," he said, finally. "I can understand."

FOUR ————————————————

AT ONE-THIRTY, Khadaji went to his rooms. The Reflex was mostly gone, but there was enough of the drug in his system to keep him awake for a couple of hours, if he'd let it. Instead, he took three hundred milligrams of parame-thaqualone—Paco, it was called in the pub—and stretched out on the bed. There were more potent sleeping medications, but a Paco would sometimes stop the nightmares that usually went with Reflex. Sometimes.

—twenty-five years old and Sub-Lojt, with a good shot at promotion to full Lojtnant, if he would sign for another tour this far in advance. A man could do worse than the military, and six years in the Jumptroops with two Distinguished Service lines on Nazo and a third for the Kontrau'lega Break would set him up for a fast track to his own centplex. That's what they told him and he had no reason to believe any different. As soon as the little scrap on Maro was done, he could come and see the Old Man's sub and talk fine points and was he interested?

Emile Khadaji nodded and grinned. He was young and understood life in the ranks. It wasn't dull, there were plenty of people who shared the places with him, he had good times with women and even a few men, he had stads to buy what he wanted. Was he interested? Yeah, he was interested—

"—see the way the fish swim through that funnel, Emile? It's plenty big enough to pass through, but once they're on the other side, they never can seem to find the narrow exit to get back out."

The boy nodded at his father and watched the fifty kilo grouper swim around inside the trap. There were five or six of the big blue-gray fish flippering back and forth. "They're stupid," he said. "The hole in the middle is the same size on both sides."

Hamay Khadaji looked down at his ten-year-old son, then back through the glass walls of the observation tank. "No, son, they aren't stupid, no more than any other fish. It's the way they look at things. It has to do with the space around them, with the way their eyes and minds work. Just because somebody or something doesn't look at the world the way you do doesn't mean it's stupid. It's just different—"

"—oh, yes, Emile, put it in, I'm ready!"

He looked down the length of Jeda's naked body, slick with sweat, at her widespread legs and damp pubic hair. He was ready too, but he wasn't sure of just what to do. Should he just plunge in all at once? Or should he move slowly? She said she liked it all at once, but the instruction tapes said it was better to be easy, gentle and—she decided for him, as he poised himself over her, by grabbing his ass with both hands and pulling him into her, hard. Oh, yes! This was wonderful, he couldn't believe how good it felt, only it wasn't going to last long, he felt himself about to explode—

—exploded into a shower of blood and torn flesh as the slugs from his carbine smacked into her flesh. The look of surprise on her face, of puzzlement, touched him. She had not known she could be hurt, that she could die. It was there on her face as she fell, the amazement. Among the hundreds of them charging across the harvested wheat field, he saw her face clearly. But the look was on other faces in the background. Wrong, the look said. This isn't right, this isn't the way it's supposed to be, those dying expressions said—

"Khadaji, get your quad to the left, three hundred degrees! There's another wave coming!"

"Jasper, Wilks, Reno, the Lojt says cover three hundred, stat!"

"Why are they still coming, Emile?" Reno was almost sobbing. "We're blowing them to fuck and they ain't even armed! They're fucking crazy!"

"Goddamn fanatics," Jasper cut in. "They don't think they can die, their leader's told them they're invincible. Well, we'll show the stupid ratholes—" He triggered another blast of his carbine, waving it back and forth at hip level like a water hose. Three hundred meters out, four or five of the attackers went down, human wheat in the field used to grow a different crop.

"Stupid fuckers, stupid fuckers, stupid, stupid—!" Jasper screamed as he fanned his weapon back and forth. All around them, other quads burned the air with blasts from their carbines, firing a locust-cloud of explosive bullets at the oncoming enemy. Thousands of the attackers dropped, so many they were stacked two or three meters high in places, with others climbing the hills of human debris to keep coming. Those were cut down as well, until the mounds of dead grew higher still.

"Why don't they stop?" Reno was crying, pointing his empty carbine at the sea of people, clicking the firing stud over and over. "Why don't they stop? Why?"

Khadaji felt gray, he felt as if a barrel of sand had been poured over him, ground into his eyes and nose and mouth and muscles. His arms ached from the weight of the carbine, the stink of electrochem propellant filled his nostrils, the roar of the explosions seemed continuous, even through the mute-plugs in his ears. But he kept firing. And firing. And firing. . . .

He opened his eyes suddenly, but otherwise didn't move. The sheets were damp from his sweat and he felt chilled. Only a dream, he told himself. Just a bad dream. He couldn't even remember it, only that it was bad. He took a couple of deep breaths and went through a relaxation drill, but he was still tense. And awake.

After a few minutes, he sat up, then stepped out of the bed. He padded across the floor, the air cool on his naked skin. He bent and touched his toes, straightened and leaned back, stretching his belly muscles. He was in good shape, but using Reflex drained him. He always resolved to avoid the stuff after he went through one of these nights, but sometimes it was necessary. Only a little while more and he could stop.

He went to his desk, slid it aside, and opened the secret store box under the flooring. In one corner was a small case, a flash-rigged packet coded to open by the print of his left ring finger. He sat cross-legged and naked on the floor by the desk and printed the lock open. Anybody who tried to violate the packet without the proper print would be rewarded by a face full of phosphoreme at 800 degrees C.

Inside the case was a writing nib and a small pad of paper. A single number was written on the top sheet: 2376. He stared at the number for a minute, then tore the sheet from the pad. Add four in the woods. Plus two on the picket line, that's six. Four more in front of the T-plex made ten and the Sub-Befal made it eleven. Twenty-three-eighty-seven. He wrote the number on the blank top sheet. He put the pad back into its case and tucked it back into the locked case. There was no need to count the flechettes, but he pulled the magazines from the two spetsdöds he'd used and double-checked them. He'd canned two of the weapons after the station in the woods, but he'd kept the ammunition. He counted the remainder of those plus the ones he'd used later. Each magazine held twelve darts, so he should have, let's see, minus two each from the first station, then two more, one from the left, one from the right. . . .

He finished the count. One short. Had he miscounted?

He closed his eyes and replayed the stations slowly. The first one was okay, the second was right, it must be the third. . . .

He fired twice, caught Jason and the quad leader with the first two rounds, then fired both his handguns again. He got Janie, but missed Toomie. . . .

Ah. Yes. He'd missed the last quadman with his first shot, it had taken a second dart for him. Khadaji grinned wryly. He was getting careless. He reached up and pulled open one of the drawers in his desk. There was a second flash-rigged packet nestled in the corner, under a banded packet of standards. A thief who opened the drawer would see the money and likely not worry about the plastic packet under it. If he or she did try to open the case, there would be a hot surprise waiting; the thief would be lucky to escape with hands and face intact.

He removed the second case from the drawer and printed it open. Inside were loose spetsdöd darts; there had been a hundred of them. Ninety-three now, Khadaji knew. He had removed seven of them in five-odd months, once for each wasted dart he'd fired. There was a pair of tweezers inside the lid of the box and he used them to pick up a single dart, which he carefully loaded into the magazine of his right-hand spetsdöd. There.

He closed the flash-rigged packet and put it back into the drawer. His carelessness hadn't been in missing Toomie, though that was bad enough; no, the problem was in forgetting that he'd missed. True, it had been in the middle of a heated exchange, but it was inexcusable.

He put the weapons away and closed the store box. There was no rigged lock on the store box itself, even though a determined search of the cubicle would likely turn it up. That was all right, it was unlikely anybody would be in here while Khadaji was alive and if he were dead, well. . . .

He suddenly felt very tired. The Reflex had finally worn off and the Paco was still pulling at him. He stood and walked back to his bed. So very tired.

He slept again, and if he dreamed, those dreams didn't disturb him.

"Good morning, Boss."

Khadaji nodded at Bork, the largest of his bouncers, one of the largest men on Greaves. Bork was of Homomue stock, from a world where the gravity was higher than normal and increased muscle mass was an asset. Here on Greaves, where the gravity was close to standard, Bork resorted to weight-lifting to keep in tone. He could have simply used elec-trostim but Bork preferred the barbells. More organic, he said.

"Bork. Things peaceful last night after I turned in?"

"Yessir. I had to warn a trooper to quiet down, but he

didn't cause any trouble after that."

Khadaji smiled. Bork was soft-spoken most of the time, but when he "warned" somebody, it could involve lifting them by the shirtfront with one hand until they were eye-level. He had seen Bork load a flexsteel bar with 275 kilos and then proceed to bench press it ten times; Bork himself weighed a good hundred and twenty-five kilos and stood close to two meters high. Most troopers smiled nervously when Bork passed.

"You're off at eight?"

"Supposed to be," Bork said, "but Sleel had to see the medic so I said I'd cover for him."

"Sleel sick?"

The larger man looked uncomfortable. "Sir. Sort of."

Khadaji didn't say anything, but he continued to stare at Bork. Finally, Bork shook his head and said, "You know how Sleel is, he thinks God created him personally to show the galaxy how to use a cock."

"He caught another exotic kind of veedee?"

"Not this time. He—uh—bet one of the girls he could outlast her."

Khadaji shook his head. "Even full of Android to the eyes he couldn't manage that. Who'd he bet?"

"Uh . . . I'm not supposed to . . . ah, hell, it was Sister Clamp."

Khadaji laughed and shook his head again. "Not really?"

"Yessir. Really."

"I would have liked to see that—after an hour or two. What's he being treated for, blisters? Or exhaustion?"

"Sister says it's something called flea-bite-us."

"Phlebitis?"

"Yessir. She says it's irritated blood vessels, an inflammation of the veins. In his—ah—dick."

"Is Sister a medic?"

"She says she used to be a doctor, but even if she wasn't,

she'd seen enough cases of this to know what it was."

Khadaji laughed again. "I'll bet she has. Poor Sleel. Maybe he learned something."

"I don't think so, Boss. He's talking about a rematch."

"Let me know if it happens, Bork. I'll bet my money on Sister."

The big man grinned. "Yessir, me too."

The octagon was about three-quarters full, early morning being the slackest period, but there were still almost two hundred men and women perched on the stools, smoking or drinking or wrapped in the grip of some other rec-chem. It could be noon or midnight, from the artificial lighting; it always looked the same in the octagon.

Khadaji looked at the scene with some fondness. As pubs went, this was one of the better ones he'd worked in—and he'd been in no small number. It would not be too hard to see himself growing old here, serving the troopers, being well thought of by the military and locals, playing this simple game. He shook his head. No. It was a nice fantasy, but that's all it was and he knew it. It was temporary, and he was better off keeping short-timer's attitude about it. There were some good people here, a lot of them, and he would miss them, but this wasn't his karmic destiny.

Lojtnant Subru entered the octagon from the front and strode across the room toward the dispensing window. He was a man in a hurry.

Khadaji walked toward the window, so that by the time Subru had bought and collected his flickstick, the owner of the Jade Flower was standing next to him.

"Something, Lojt?"

Subru scratched the end of the flickstick along the seam of his creased uniform pants. The tip flared, then faded to a glowing dot. He stuck the flickstick to his lips and drew in a deep breath of the fragrant smoke. He held the blast

for a second, then began to speak. Dark purple smoke
emerged from his mouth with the words. "A major attack,
Emile. The Scum hit a T-plex last night. *My* T-plex. They
got the guards and then hit the C.O. herself." He took
another hit from the stick. "*I* could have been there. If
they'd come a day earlier, I would have been sitting on the
O.O.D. desk my-fucking-self."

"They get any of the rebels?"

"Not alive. I hear there were twenty-five or thirty of the
Scum involved in the attack. Armed with stolen .177s and
spetsdöds."

"The troops ought to be wearing class two or three armor,
Subbie."

The Lojt glanced at Khadaji's face through the smoke.
He seemed more relaxed, now. "There's not enough to go
around. You were in the Quartermasters, you know how
Supply works. In a ten-kay, you only get so many suits and
additional reqs take months. Besides, class two won't stop
a .177 and you can't move in class three except to waddle."

"Way I heard it, most of the casualties are from dart
poison, so class two should—"

"Where did you hear that?" Even through the drug, he
sounded suspicious. Careful, Khadaji told himself.

"I run a pub, Subbie. I hear a lot of things. Men get
drunk or stoned, they say things they don't think about."

Subru shook his head. "Damn! Listen, Emile, I know
this won't get past you, but upranks is shitting bricks over
this thing. A lot of the troops the Scum have hit are stiffies
from Spasm poisoning and some of them *were* wearing class
two. I even heard of a couple wearing class three who took
darts."

"I don't believe it." He knew that was not true, he wasn't
so stupid he'd try a class three with a spetsdöd.

"My information comes from high places, Emile. But if
you hear any of the troops babbling in their smoke or splash,

see if you can't shut them up before they get their asses into a sharp crack. The Old Man would love to have a target to shoot at, any target, including our own."

"Okay, Subbie, I'll try and keep your boys out of trouble in my place. It would be bad for business if somebody thought they talked too much in here and made me off-limits."

"Thanks, Emile. I appreciate it."

Khadaji left the shaken Lojtnant inhaling flickstick smoke and walked for the closest exit. He needed some unpolluted air. Sometimes, this game seemed to get too twisty, even for him. But Lojtnant Subru was in Administration, he had access to all the facts about the campaign against the Shamba Scum and he believed that the rebels were able to knock off men in class three body armor with spetsdöds, something Khadaji himself knew was impossible.

It was twisty, but it was going better than he'd hoped.

And the end was nearly here.

FIVE ————————————————

SLEEL'S PHLEBITIS MUST have responded to treatment, Khadaji thought, because the bouncer was working the floor, watching for signs of trouble from the crowd in the Jade Flower. It was quiet, though. Butch had run out of midrange sops and had, reluctantly, begun offering the highrange chemical at the same price. Soldiers loved a bargain, and a lot of them were barely awake at their tables, stoked with the glow of the depressant drug. Nobody fought on high-sops, it took more energy than a user had available.

Anjue gave him the news when Khadaji went to check on the line.

"Have you heard about quadman Pendragon?"

"I don't believe I know a trooper by that name."

The doormaster waved his hands. "He was one of the first—if not *the* first—hit by the Shamba Freedom Forces. Six months ago, it was."

Khadaji nodded. "So?"

"He's awake. The first to recover from the poisoning."

"Ah."

"Good news, eh?"

"Indeed."

He wandered back into the octagon, thinking. So. The first one was out of it. He tried to remember the earliest troopers he'd stationed. They all seemed to run together, it was hard to pick out a single man or woman. There were some who stuck in his memory, of course: the couple drinking contraband vöremhölts in the swirltub; the trooper who covered his face with his hands and would spend the months that way; the two nude women who came at him with knives. There were so many of them, though, he couldn't summon up, they were just bodies falling, locked in tetany. But they were coming back to their interrupted lives, now. Quadman Pendragon may or may not have seen him. Probably not— he'd been particularly careful in the beginning, sometimes wearing skinmasks, sometimes shooting from hiding. But not always. They would start awakening by the dozens pretty soon, and some of them had seen him. Some of them had known who he was. Very shortly, the game was going to be over. Now it would get tricky, it could all fall apart if he allowed it to go too far.

Khadaji found he was breathing faster, that his heart was rumbling along quicker than normal. Funny. He had known this was coming and yet now that it was here, he felt a thrill of fear running through him like some electric current. The years of mind and body training, of mental and physical control kicked in, and he calmed himself. He slowed his pulse and breathing, but the hormone balance was not so easy. The chemicals were stirred and it took more than a quick effort of will to smooth those waters. Later, he would go to his cube and spend a few minutes meditating, that would do it. He needed a clear mind for what was to come.

• • •

One more station. It would be dangerous, maybe foolishly so. The big holoproj was hardly over—it was only just started—but this portion of it was coming to a close. Khadaji had mixed emotions about it. On the one hand, there was the fear—he could end it all now if he screwed it up. On the other hand, if he pulled it off, it would be the final touch, a major coup. And it was the last. If it worked, it would serve and if it failed, well, there were risks in everything. As Subru had put it, one could be flattened by a ground-effect tank while crossing the street. Life was always shadowed by death.

Preparations were simple. Khadaji took the container of extra spetsdöd darts from his desk, along with the writing pad with the number of casualties from the hidden box under his desk and dropped them into a public disposal. There was a flash as the unit's lasers ignited the rigged packets. The disposal was built to take worse and now that evidence was gone. If nothing else, the legend was safe.

He walked back to the Jade Flower and used the public com just outside the fresher. As he waited for the connection to be made, he looked around, taking in the sights and sounds and smells of the pub. It was all very sharp, diamond-clear, made so he realized by the fact this might be the last time he would see it. Interesting how a man's mind worked—

"Befalhavare Creg's office."

Khadaji turned his attention to the com. "This is Emile Khadaji, owner of the Jade Flower. I'd like to speak to the Befalhavare."

"Hold, sir, I'll get the Sub—"

"Negative, mister. I need the Old Man himself."

"Sir, Befalhavare Creg is in conference at the moment and cannot be disturbed. If you would like to leave a message, you will be contacted when—"

"Listen, mister, I am holding 'Ears Only' material for

your C.O. You don't want to be the one who kept him from hearing it ASAP."

There was a pause. Khadaji could imagine the soldier's thoughts. There were procedures, standing orders which were supposed to be followed. Deviation from such could mean his ass; on the other hand, if Khadaji—a man of some local standing—was holding 'Ears Only' material and wasn't put through, the Old Man might use somebody's balls for marbles. Either way was a risk. It would depend upon how bright the clerk was.

He was bright. "Hold a moment, sir, I'll put you through."

Khadaji grinned into the comset.

The Old Man was not one to waste words. "What?"

"Befalhavare Creg, Emile Khadaji, I'm the owner—"

"I know who you are, sir. What is your business rattling my clerk?"

Khadaji smiled again. "I know who the leaders of the Shamba Forces are."

"I'll send a quad for you, stay where you are."

Naturally, Khadaji thought, the call would be traced, but it wasn't going to be played that way. "I would rather not be a target," Khadaji said. "I'll get to your office on my own. But if word gets out, I'm a dead man. This is between the two of us, no one else."

"My word," Befal Creg said.

"I am on my way."

Khadaji's grin broadened as he broke the connection. The Old Man would be scrambling already, getting stress analyzers set up, recorders checked, drugs and electropophy gear brought to his office. A commander of ten thousand men would hardly be careless when it involved something this major. Khadaji expected no less. By the time he left the Jade Flower, probably a dozen quads would have been com-dispatched to collect him.

The first quad found him within two minutes. Another joined for backup. Five men and three women formed a circle around Khadaji and escorted him to the Befalhavare's office, alert for any attacks by the Shamba Scum. Khadaji allowed himself a short laugh.

The security at the C.O.'s office was impressive. Fifty troopers, half in class three armor, and a ground-effect spin-gun guarded the building. The Scum weren't going to storm this building. Khadaji kept his face impassive as he was marched into the hardfoam structure. Of course, the Scum didn't have to storm the building. . . .

Khadaji was checked for weapons; he emptied his pockets—he only had a pack of flicksticks and some change, which he handed to the Lojt in charge—was hand-searched, then walked past a fluroproj to double check that he had no material secreted in his clothes or body cavities.

"Clean," the tech said, looking at the proj.

The Lojt handed the flicksticks and money back to Khadaji. Khadaji extended the pack toward the officer. "Like a smoke?"

"No, sir. Not on duty."

"For later, maybe?"

The officer hesitated a moment, then shook his head. "Better not. Go ahead in, sir."

Inside, there was at least a pretense of privacy; Creg sat behind his desk, and the two men were alone in the room.

"Sit," Creg ordered.

Khadaji shook his head. "First we make sure I get back to the Jade Flower alive," he said. "I want you to arrange for a quad to escort me back, now that you've marked me by having me brought in under heavy guard."

"It'll be taken care of."

"No, sir. I want you to get on the com and tell that friendly Lojt outside the door that when I come out, he's to take me back to the Flower without any stops—that anybody who tries to approach is probably Scum, no matter what they claim to be or look like and they are to be spiked."

The commanding officer of the forces on Greaves looked irritated. "Mister Khadaji, you have vital information for me and we are under Military Interdiction. I can pry what I want from you in five minutes."

"I know that," Khadaji said. Careful. "But I'm here voluntarily. I want to tell you what I know, and you can verify it easily. I just want to make sure I survive. Is it so unreasonable a request?"

Befalhavare Creg weighed his options. Khadaji could see him decide. "All right, Mister Khadaji." He reached for the com unit on his desk, touched a pressure-sensitive pad, and spoke quietly. "Temms, when this man leaves here, you are to escort him back to where he came from. No one is to approach without being considered an assassin—not anyone, including your mother, you copy?"

"Sir."

The Old Man looked up. He was only about fifty, Khadaji estimated, hardly old, with a military shag cut and hard features. Probably a by-the-tape commander.

"You have somebody monitoring this conversation, commander?"

"I gave you my word otherwise, didn't I?"

"Recording?"

"That I do, mister. Now, you had something to tell me?"

Khadaji nodded. He took the pack of flicksticks from his pocket. "Do you mind if I smoke?"

Creg shook his head. "Not if you get to the point."

Khadaji smiled and scratched the tip of the flickstick along the leg of his pants. The tip flared and he put the doped cigarette to his lips, but didn't draw on it.

"Me," Khadaji said.

"Excuse me?"

"Me. I'm the leader of the Shamba Freedom Forces. In fact, I'm the whole army."

Creg's eyes widened, then narrowed. "I don't much care for jokes, mister—!"

Khadaji took a deep breath, centered the flickstick in his mouth, and blew, hard. There was a paper tube inside the thinly packed flickstick and inside the tube, a single dart of fluroproj-transparent plastic, just in case. The dart tore through the tip of the smoldering flickstick and across the desk, hitting Befalhavare Creg's throat. The poison took him, one knee snapping up into his desk, throwing him forward. Number twenty-three-eighty-eight, Khadaji thought. He wouldn't be able to top this one.

He stood and walked to the door, slid it aside and was out. He locked the door behind him. The Lojtnant looked startled.

"Time to go," Khadaji said.

"That didn't take long."

Khadaji shrugged. "Who are we to question the C.O.?"

"I should check with him—"

"I wouldn't. He told me he wanted a few minutes to think about what I told him. No calls short of planetary emergency, I think he said."

The Lojt nodded. "All right. This way."

It would take five minutes to get back to the Jade Flower; it would probably be another twenty or thirty minutes after that before anybody seriously tried to disturb Befalhavare Creg; there would be another few minutes of confusion after he was found before the chain-of-command collected itself enough to check the recording and figure out what happened; finally, a few more minutes would elapse before troopers stormed the Jade Flower, looking for the Shamba Scum. He could figure on an hour, at least. Plenty of time.

Inside the Flower, Khadaji found Sleel. "Clear everybody out," he said. "We're closing."

"Huh?"

"The Jade Flower is going to close. Tell Anjue to start herding the troops out; I want the place cleared in fifteen minutes."

"But—but—"

"Just do it." Khadaji was aware of Sleel's stare at his back as he walked toward the drug room. He rapped on the densecris window and got Butch's attention.

"What's happenin', Boss?"

"Open up, Butch."

The reaper locks snicked open and the thick stainless steel door swung wide. The chief pubtender stood in the doorway. "Somethin' up?"

"Go help Sleel. We're closing for a little while. I want everybody outside."

"What's the deal?"

"Not to worry, Butch. Somebody will be asking for me soon—tell them where I am." He walked into the drug room and started to cycle the door shut.

"What is it, Boss? You in some kinda trouble? Listen, me 'n' Sleel can hold 'em off if you—"

Khadaji smiled. "Thanks, Butch, I appreciate it. But you do what I told you, that'll help the most." The door swung closed. Khadaji walked over in front of the dispensing window and stood framed in it. He saw Butch and Sleel both look at him, and at least a dozen troopers saw him before he opaqued the window. The crystal faded slowly to black.

Alone in the room, he took a deep breath and slowly sat on his heels in the kneeling position called *seiza*. He had at least three-quarters of an hour, plenty of time for a short meditation.

His mind would not be still. It had been over ten years

since he'd learned the first of the calming procedures he'd used from that point. They had become almost automatic in that time, his control was nearly perfect. Zazen, kuji-kiri, throndu, point-contraction, mantra, mandala—he knew them all, cages for the monkey brain. But the monkey was elusive this time. And it had a larger, fiercer cousin, a beast which slept in a deep and black cave in the back of Khadaji's mind. The monkey's nervous chattering of doom awoke the shaggy creature. Death? It said, red eyes narrowing. No. I will fight Death and kill him! I am not ready to die. Never.

Khadaji sighed. Too many years, too much preparation had gone into this; too much was stirred for him to calm himself now. Instead of being lulled, his mind was preter-naturally alert, filled with thoughts and desires and mem-ories. He saw quietly, but his head was full of storm; epinepherine surged through his blood and washed over his shores in pounding waves. Khadaji remembered.

He remembered it all.

SIX ─────────────────

THE WOMAN EXPLODED into a shower of blood and torn flesh as the slugs from his carbine smacked into her. The look of surprise on her face, of puzzlement, touched him. She had not known she could be hurt, that she could die. It was there on her face as she fell, the amazement. Among the thousands of them charging across the harvested wheat field, Khadaji saw her face clearly. But the look was on other faces in the background. Wrong, the look said. This isn't right, this isn't the way it's supposed to be, those dying expressions said—

"Khadaji, get your quad to the left, three hundred degrees! There's another wave coming!"

"Jasper, Wilks, Reno, the Lojt says cover three hundred, stat!"

"Why are they still coming, Emile?" Reno was almost sobbing. "We're blowing them to fuck and they ain't even armed! They're fucking crazy!"

47

"Goddamn fanatics," Jasper cut in. "They don't think they can die, their leader's told them they're invincible. Well, we'll show the stupid ratholes—" He triggered another blast of his carbine, waving it back and forth at hip level like a water hose. Three hundred meters out, four or five of the attackers went down, human wheat in the field used to grow a different crop.

"Stupid fuckers, stupid fuckers, stupid, stupid—!" Jasper screamed as he fanned his weapon back and forth. All around them, other quads burned the air with blasts from their carbines, firing a locust-cloud of explosive bullets at the oncoming enemy. Thousands of the attackers dropped, so many they were stacked two or three meters high in places, with others climbing the hills of human debris to keep coming. Those were cut down as well, until the mounds of dead grew higher still—

"Why don't they stop?" Reno was crying, pointing his empty carbine at the sea of people, clicking the firing stud over and over. "Why don't they stop? Why?"

Khadaji felt gray, he felt as if a barrel of sand had been poured over him, ground into his eyes and nose and mouth and muscles. His arms ached from the weight of the carbine, the stink of electrochem propellant filled his nostrils, the roar of the explosions seemed continuous, even through the mute-plugs in his ears. But he kept firing. And firing. And firing. . . .

—exploded into a shower of blood and torn flesh—

"—your quad to the left, three hundred degrees—!"

"—Goddamn fanatics—!"

"—stupid fuckers, stupid, stupid—!"

Khadaji turned away from the slaughter and dropped into a squat over the dry ground; he ejected the magazine from his weapon, drew a full one from his belt and clicked it into place. The sensors in the carbine noted the load. There was a quiet whine as the first round cycled into the firing chamber. He felt as if he had been dipped in lead; the smallest movement was hard, straightening and turning took the energy of a ten klick run. He moved in slow motion, a man standing in thick lube gel to his neck. He pointed his weapon in the general direction of the attackers—there was no need to aim—and triggered it. The Parker carbine vibrated in his hands, sending explosive bullets to join the killing. It seemed to him as if he'd been born to this foreign world, as if he'd lived his whole life here, firing and loading and firing and loading and firing, as if he would surely grow old and die here. His chronometer must have stopped, it showed that only an hour had passed since the first wave of fanatics—yes, Jasper was right—fanatics had swept toward the foam-blocked positons of the Confed's Jump-troops. Only an hour? He had never fired for a solid hour before. Sometime during that period, a supply robot had issued him a new weapon; dozens of the anodized aluminum dins ran back and forth behind the line, dropping new belts of loaded magazines and replacing burned-out weapons, so the firepower would not slacken.

And still they came. There must be millions of them, he had never seen so many people in one place, all moving with such singleness of purpose. They weren't even *armed!* The dead were piled into mounds of warm flesh, there had to be two or three hundred thousand of them covering the field, withering lower under the explosive spray of a ten kay at full throttle.

Why? Why did they walk into certain death, never pausing?

His weapon clicked dry. Mechanically, he turned, squatted, and reloaded. The machinery of his carbine whined again, telling him it was ready.

Why are we killing these people?

Khadaji stared at his weapon. The barrel was hot, smoke rose from it in thin tendrils into the cooler air. The weapon seemed alien, suddenly, a strange instrument whose function he couldn't understand. The gravity was a standard gee, the air carried enough oxy, but this was not his world. The bright yellow sun was hotter than his own; the smells of planet Maro were different from those of San Yubi. Ten thousand of the Confederation's finest had been bent here, to spend ammunition and time target shooting.

No. Those weren't targets out there. He was shooting people, people who laughed and cried and ate and fucked and he was killing them. In the name of any god which might have ever existed, *why?* What could justify that? What had they done to deserve to die? Because they opposed the confed? Because the confed wanted order on this world? It was insane!

"Khadaji, what's up? Your weapon jammed?"

The voice of the centplex's commander, Lojtnant Hogan, blared from the transceiver over Khadaji's left ear.

"Jammed?" The word was as meaningless as the chunk of deadly plastic, spun crystal and metal that he held.

But the Lojt misunderstood. "Supply is on the way. Hold on for a minute."

Khadaji became aware of his breathing. The damped noise of the constant firing faded from his consciousness; the yelling of the troopers dwindled, the screams of the dying trailed off, and all he could hear was his own breathing. In, out, a little hoarse, but it was steady. His heartbeat was slow, a gently throb under his skin. He felt as if he'd been wrapped in a thick blanket, he was warm, comfortable and alone. He stood slowly and turned yet slower, to look at the sea of dead and about-to-be-dead.

Why?

Because.

The invisible blanket was removed. All the sounds and sights and smells and tastes came back in a rush. The stink of death, of explosives, the cries, the blood. Everything burst upon him in that moment. He *knew!* He understood *why!* He could not have said it, there were no words, but the Realization burst from his innermost being. It was all right. ALL RIGHT! Not good, not moral, but he *understood* it, all in a single cosmic flash which lasted only a second. It was more potent than any psychedelic he'd ever taken, stronger than anything he'd ever felt. Emile Antoon Khadaji suddenly and without any logical or apparent reason knew just who he was, exactly what his place in the universe was. He knew who he was, and so he knew too what he must do.

He grinned and put his left hand on the top block of foam, then vaulted over it and began to run toward the approaching mob. The sunshine warmed him; the smells were fine, now.

"Buddha! Emile, what the fuck are you doing—?"

"—Khadaji, get back here—!"

"—pull your fire or you'll hit him—!"

"—slipped his drive—!"

As he ran, Khadaji tore the transceiver from his ear and tossed it away. The voices from the radio went with it. The explosive bullets screamed and whined past him, but they didn't matter. He would be hit or he wouldn't, it was all the same, it didn't matter in the overall scheme of things, whatever was right would happen. . . .

A tumbling bullet nicked his left boot, ripping the heel away, and he stumbled, tripped and fell. He managed to turn the fall into a shoulder roll, came up and kept running. Without the heel, it was a lopsided run, he nearly fell again, but he kept going. He was fifty meters out and nearing the first of the dead. Another fifty meters and he would be there—

A body near him jumped under the impact of a slug and an arm blew away from the corpse and bounced from Khadaji's chest as he ran. He didn't slow. He could see the faces of the attackers now, dull, almost like plastic dolls, showing no fear or emotion as they moved toward their goal. They didn't have a chance of reaching it, of course, he knew that. They would learn it as they died; only then would the vapid expressions change in sudden surprise.

He passed the first of them. They ignored him. His uniform seemed to make no difference, they could not focus on a single man. He began to strip the lightweight gear away, still running.

When he was down to a thin coverall, he finally slowed to a walk. There were still thousands, tens of thousands, hundreds of thousands of them, all moving opposite the way he now walked. Those in front of him moved to let him pass, as if they knew he was a man with a mission, as if they could somehow see he was a man on fire.

He walked on, not knowing where he would go, what exactly he would do, only that he was going to do *some*thing. He had no money, no way to get off the world, no way to live. He had known only the military and he was done with that now. But he didn't worry. He had no cares and no problem was too big for him to solve, he knew he had the answers somewhere within him, he had only to look.

Somewhere within him, he would find a plan.

SEVEN ─────────────────

THE MEMORY OF it was still strong as he wandered about
the streets of Notzeerath. A few kilometers away, three-
quarters of a million people had died violently only days
earlier, but there was no sign of it here. There was no fear
of the Void in these people, he understood that now. They
were believers in soul regeneration, of being born anew
after each cycle. Their High Priest was considered a god
and they would march into the teeth and claws of death for
him. Many had. More would. Khadaji was wrapped in his
personal Realization still, and so he understood. He knew
whatever answers he needed would come to him—he was
operating totally on an intuitive level for the first time in
his life. He didn't worry about the Military looking for him.
They would surely think he was dead—walking into the
fanatics as he had, he should have been torn to pieces. They
wouldn't even look for his body, among all the others. He
stood on a corner, awash in the sensual input of the city:

six-wheeled vehicles with alcohol-powered engines rumbled
by on hard plastic tires; people shopped at an open-air fruit
and vegetable market; the steady thrum of a broadcast generator vibrated from the plastcrete through his bare feet. He
had thrown his boots away.

"Lost, pilgrim?" came a deep voice from behind him.

Khadaji turned, to see a figure wrapped from head to
foot in folds of gray cloth. Only the eyes and hands were
visible in the gray cloud. The eyes were green and clear,
the hands short-fingered and powerful looking, ridged with
tendons and thick veins. A man's hands. He must be hot
under all that material, Khadaji thought.

Khadaji smiled. "Lost? No. I don't know where I am,
but I'm not lost."

The man in gray laughed. "A zen answer, pilgrim, and
perfect for a holy man. Have you been such long?"

"I'm not a holy man," he said. "Until a few days ago,
I was a soldier. Something . . . happened. I . . . saw something, felt something, somehow. A vision."

The tall figure in gray nodded. "Ah. *Relampago*. You
are blessed, pilgrim."

Khadaji didn't know the word; however, he was certain
that the man was going to tell him what it meant.

He did. "The Cosmic Flash, the Existential Lightning,
the Finger of God—*Relampago*. There are people who labor
a lifetime hoping for that touch, sweating through postures
and prayers and complex rituals."

"I'm not sure that's what happened to me—"

"Oh, it is, pilgrim. It shows. You are producing psychic
energy like a kirlian flare. Anyone with any sensitivity could
see it. Even a blind man could feel it through the pores of
his skin." The man in gray shook his head and Khadaji
knew he was smiling, even though he could not see his
face. "I'm the current Pen," he said, "and this tent I wear

marks me as a member of the Holy Order of the Siblings of the Shroud."

"You're a priest?"

"Close enough. It's a bit more complicated than that, but the designation is sufficient."

Khadaji thought for a few seconds. "You said you were the current Pen. Is that a name or a title?"

"My name. Pens come and Pens go, and it is my lot to be the Pen of the moment. When I am gone, another will take the name and carry on. There is never more than one of us at a time."

Khadaji understood. A week ago, it would have sounded weird, but now it made perfect sense. Though he couldn't have said why, exactly, he knew it did.

"What can I do for you, then, Pen?"

Pen moved his hands so that the palms faced the sky. "It is I who is to do for you, pilgrim."

"My name is Khadaji. Emile Khadaji."

"Ah. Well, Emile Khadaji, I am, among other things, a teacher. Can you tell me of your vision?"

Khadaji smiled. He shook his head. "There are no words for the feeling," he said. "The best I have come up with is that I felt and heard and saw and smelled and tasted a sense of . . . rightness. Of order, of unfolding as it should be."

"Ah. And how did this vision come to be?"

Khadaji told Pen of the slaughter. He left none of it out. When he finished, the gray-robed figure nodded.

"Yes. It happens that way. Would you care to hear the psychology and physiology of the experience? The science of it?"

Before Khadaji could speak, Pen continued. "Oh. Excuse me, I forget my manners. You need new clothes, and food. When did you eat last?"

Khadaji considered it. "Three days," he said. "Before

the attack. I've been drinking water from public fountains, but food hasn't seemed very important."

The fabric covering Pen's face shifted slightly. He had to be smiling. "Come, then, we'll see to clothing and food and then we'll talk."

While it somehow seemed natural that Pen would do these things for him, Khadaji felt a sense of wonder about it. Before he could ask, Pen answered his question. "When one is ready for a teacher, a teacher appears; the same is true of students—when the right one appears, a teacher knows. The Disk spins and we are spiraled along to our proper places. It was no chance which brought us together this day, Emile Khadaji, but the twirlings of the Disk—for now, we are for each other."

Khadaji nodded. He had never paid court to mysticism, he had been raised by atheist parents and shaped by a pragmatic military, but he was no longer the person he had been. He followed the bulky figure in gray because he understood, in some strange fashion, what Pen meant.

They sat in the shade, under a broad-leafed pulse tree in the court of an outdoor restaurant. Khadaji now wore a set of loose-weave orthoskins in a gray which nearly matched Pen's shroud, and dotic boots custom-spun for his feet. He ate slowly from a plate of highly-spiced vegetables and sipped from a mug of splash. Arteries throbbed under the woody skin of the pulse tree a meter away. He watched them and listened while he ate.

Pen was talking. Lecturing. "The psychology of the religious experience has been well-researched and taped. There are many paths up the mountain—sensory deprivation or sensory overload—emotional response to stimuli or the lack thereof is common. Drugs, of course, from psychoactives to the more mundane depressants. Electropophy can bring it about, as can organic brain damage, lack or excess of oxygen, even sex can trigger it. And what it is, according to the science of man and mue, is a subjective mental state, somewhere to the left of hypnosis. A trick the mind plays on itself. A delusion, void of reality."

Khadaji took another bite of the vegetables, then grinned.

Pen inclined his head slightly to one side. "And none of what I've just said matters at all, does it?"

Khadaji shrugged. "I know what I felt. I hear what you are saying. I understand it here—" he tapped his head with one finger, "—but that doesn't compare to the way I feel it *here*." He pointed at his belly.

"You are convinced of its truth?"

Khadaji nodded.

"Good. So am I. Science, alas, for all it has done for us, is sometimes short-sighted. A product of the monkey-brain, science is, and too concerned with numbers and equations and limits, at times. Today's mysticism will be tomorrow's science."

Khadaji sipped at his splash. The midly alcoholic drink did little to wash the hot spices away.

"You have told me of your vision," Pen said. "You have glimpsed the Disk as it spun, the largeness of it, the rightness of it. But you saw flaws."

Khadaji sighed. "Yes. It was not so much a sight as a feeling. Everything was right, but there was a kind of . . . wrongness, as well. About man."

"A large painting is made up of many figures," Pen said. "You can see it at a distance and get an impression of it, but you cannot know it until you look closer, at the small parts which form it. The study will take some time; it may lead you to many places. I can only guide you part of the way. Will you allow me to show you what I can?"

This was part of it, Khadaji knew. He had a sense of mission, of purpose so strong he had no choice but to go with it. He nodded again. "Yes," he said.

• • •

There was a flat yard of thick grass trimmed short behind the building in which Pen had his rooms. Khadaji felt the mat sink under his dotics as he walked on it, like a plush carpet. He turned and faced Pen, who stood two meters away.

"Before you can properly influence others, you must control yourself," Pen said. "Body control is the easiest but it must be mastered. You are trained as a soldier, with weapons. And, I assume, some unarmed skills?"

"Oppugnate," Khadaji said. "Military boxing, with hands and feet."

"Good. Attack me, using your training."

Khadaji hesitated. It was hard to determine Pen's age from his hands and eyes alone, but he was easily old enough to be Khadaji's father—maybe his grandfather. "I am still circulating bacteria-aug," he said. "For another six months, until the colonies die, I will be considerably faster than an unaugmented human."

"It doesn't matter," Pen said. "Launch your attack."

Khadaji shifted into a fighting stance, left foot forward, his left hand held high, his right low, fingers extended and stiffened, thumbs curled tightly. He edged forward slightly, keeping his legs wide for balance. He had been training in the unarmed combat for nearly six years; he was young, strong, and practiced. He didn't want to hurt Pen, so he figured to snake in and tap the man lightly a couple of times and then back off. He kept his eyes impassive, focused on the entire figure, and held his breathing even, so as not to reveal his intent.

Pen stood quietly, looking relaxed, his hands by his sides.

Khadaji jumped suddenly, half again as fast as a normal man, and jabbed his stiffened hand at the other man's solar plexus; it was fast, but not hard.

Pen pivoted, caught Khadaji's wrist lightly with his thumb

and forefinger and did a kind of two-step dance, ending in a twirl. Khadaji felt himself lose balance and start to fall. He twisted and managed to roll out of the fall, but he hit the ground harder than expected; it jarred his teeth together. He came up, spun, and crouched, to face Pen again.

Pen stood as he had before, looking unconcerned.

Khadaji considered the throw. Some sort of wrestling technique, rather than boxing. All right. One of the judo or jujitsu or aikido variants. Well. That could be handled. If he kept his weight centered and only used muscle-strikes, he could avoid being thrown.

He moved in, snapping his right foot up toward Pen's groin, still fast but without real power, then stepped down and swung his hand around in a sweeping chop. His stance was solid, it was unlikely he'd be pulled off-balance at this angle.

Pen shifted, spun again and seemed to wave his hand past Khadaji's shoulder with only a light touch. Khadaji went over backwards. He reached out to slap at the soft grass with both hands, but he still hit hard, on his back. It knocked the wind from him. He twisted to one side, rolling, and scrambled up, trying to inhale tiny sips of air. Maro's sun beat upon him and he felt his face go hot. The air was heavy with moisture and sweat rolled down his neck and spine. This was all wrong. He was faster than Pen, he could feel that. Okay. The problem was in his attack. An initiated strike left one more open than defense, an attacker had to commit himself while a defender only had to wait. He would stand his ground and wait for Pen's move, then.

The two men stood facing each other for what seemed like a long time to Khadaji. He kept his stance wide and powerful, his hands raised to cover himself high and low, and waited. Pen, meanwhile, simply stood in his neutral stance.

Finally, Pen moved. He raised his hands and clasped

them together. He began to knit his fingers together in an intricate weave, crossing and uncrossing, locking and unlocking the digits in strange and complex patterns. Khadaji stared at Pen's hands. What was he—?

Pen stepped forward, almost slowly, Khadaji thought. He reached out with one foot and kicked, a kick aimed at Khadaji's leading leg, behind the knee. The younger man couldn't seem to move in time to parry or block. Pen's instep smacked solidly into Khadaji's leg, lifting it high. For the third time, Khadaji fell, arms flailing. This time, he stayed on the grass. He sat up and stared at the other man.

Pen laughed, a deep belly rumble.

Khadaji shook his head. "I suppose I'm missing something funny."

"Only a cliche," Pen said.

"I don't understand."

"This whole scene." Pen waved one arm to encompass Khadaji and the surrounding landscape. "The old martial arts master defeating the young student. It's classic. Problem with cliches is, they get to be that way because they tend to be more or less valid. I couldn't devise a better means to show you I have something you need to learn than the old routine. Sometimes older is better, it seems."

Pen bent and extended a hand to Khadaji, then helped lift him back onto his feet. "The art is called sumito," he said, "and the idea is to learn to control your own body, not defeat somebody else. When you can make your hands and feet go where you want them to, it doesn't matter if you have an opponent or not."

Khadaji shook his head. He had always been taught that muscle memory required specificity—if you wanted to learn to play nullball, you practiced in zee-gee; if you wanted to improve boxing skill, you boxed with a partner. Anything less was good only for general conditioning, not specific skills. On the other hand, Pen had been tossing him around as if he were feeble and brainless, instead of a trained and augmented professional soldier. Had to be something to what the man said. Had to be something.

EIGHT ———————————————

KHADAJI STARED AT the floor. There was a strange pattern of footsteps drawn there, laid out like some madman's dance. He looked up at Pen. "What am I supposed to do here?"

Pen smiled. "It's simple enough. Walk the pattern."

Khadaji shrugged. He began to step on the drawn figures. They seemed to be exactly the size and shape of his own feet. The first five steps were simple. He looked at the sixth with disbelief. "I can't reach that one from here."

"Certainly you can."

"Not without twisting like a contortionist, I can't."

"Try."

Khadaji tried. He kept his weight on his left foot while he stretched his right leg and attempted to twist his ankle to make his right foot conform to the diagram. He lost his balance and almost fell. "Can't do it," he said.

"No?" Pen motioned for Khadaji to stand aside. He stood at the beginning of the pattern and began to walk it. When he reached the sixth step, he simply *did* it. Khadaji wasn't sure how. One second he was facing this way, the next second, *that* way. The man was shorter, had shorter legs, and if he could stretch that far, Khadaji should be able to also.

It took nine tries before he succeeded, but Khadaji finally made the sixth step. He looked at Pen and smiled.

Pen's face was invisible within the shroud, but he did nod. "Very good. The seventh step?"

Khadaji looked down. Buddha! It was impossible, nobody could get there without falling! He glared at Pen, mentally daring him to do it.

Pen did. This time, he walked the entire pattern, almost a hundred steps. Ninety-seven, to be exact. It was a number Khadaji would grow to detest. In six weeks, he could manage to make it to step fifty. Sometimes. It was radically different than the oppugnate training he had learned in the military. It didn't seem to make any sense.

During that time, Pen began to teach Khadaji other things. They hopped around on one leg. Sat motionless for long periods. Did stretching exercises which hurt him in places Khadaji didn't even know he had. He was learning something, Khadji knew. What, he didn't know. But something.

Somewhere along the way, Khadaji began to lose the sense of foreknowledge he'd had. He still had the memory, but the sense of oneness he'd felt with the universe during the slaughter faded and became less sharp. There were some moments when he could touch it, but they became fewer and shorter. It was as if he'd passed through a magical door on a conveyer; he continued to move and the door grew smaller behind him. He wanted to stay at the portal, but he could not. And he didn't know where he was going.

So, when Pen began one particular teaching, Khadaji found himself puzzled.

They were sitting in the largest of Pen's rooms, a low-ceilinged square six meters on a side. The room was cool, despite the heat of Maro's summer outside, kept that way by a strip of lindex filter set under the opaqued window. There were three foam chairs, a desk with a comp terminal on it, and a large chest against one wall; no other furniture.

"Pubtending? Are you serious?"

Pen laughed from within the folds of his gray shroud. "To be sure," he said. "One must make a living."

Khadaji had a little trouble picturing Pen behind a bar, or window, mixing drinks and dispensing tablets. He said as much.

"Ah, but it is a perfect job for a priest, even one so unpriestly as I. Consider: who has a better opportunity to see people with their masks lowered than a pubtender? Men will confide things to you drunk they wouldn't tell a brother when sober; stoned women will reveal secrets they'd never speak as pillow talk while straight. More than one pubtender has come from the ranks of practicing psychologists—or gone there from some bar."

Khadaji shook his head. "I don't know. . . ."

Pen waved one hand. "What's to know? You'll have to do *something* to feed yourself—I won't be around forever. A top-ranked pubtender can always get a job and as I said, there are few places better to study the human condition. More, it's a skill I can teach you."

Khadaji stood and walked to the plastic window. He touched a control on the sill and the window shifted from near black to clear. The light was too bright, bringing a blast of reflectled heat with it. He darkened the window again. "Somehow, it doesn't seem exactly what I had in mind."

"And what did you have in mind?"

Khadaji turned to look at Pen. "I—I don't know. Something. . . ."

"Ah. I see. Well, until you figure out what, precisely, perhaps it would be wise to learn what is available."

Khadaji considered it. Pen was right. He only had vagueness where he felt he should have some plan. Pubtending? It was as good as anything, he supposed. And easy enough, he figured.

He was wrong about how easy it would be. He found that out quickly.

Pen stood and walked to the comp terminal. He removed a small steel marble from his robe and held it out so Khadaji could see it. Khadaji recognized the ball as a recording sphere, a storage device for information. Though the sphere was small, it would hold several hundred volumes of hard copy.

"This contains seventeen years of experience as a pubtender," Pen said. "Every drink I know how to mix, every chem, planetary and local laws regarding dispensing, favorites on different worlds, everything. Cross-referenced, indexed, annotated and illustrated. Come and see."

Pen dropped the vacuum-formed steel ball into a circular slot on the computer's terminal and stroked the unit to life. The operating system acknowledged the format of the sphere with a wash of colors and words across the holoproj image above the keyboard, then went into mode-select.

"Verbal," Pen said, "standard Interstitchi, float it."

"Acknowledged," the computer said. It had a deep, feminine voice.

"Index—categories, primo screen—give me this one visual."

"Running."

Two seconds after the computer spoke, four words splashed into the air over the unit. Khadaji blinked and stared at the projection. The words were:

LIQUIDS, SOLIDS, GASES, RADIANTS

Pen turned to Khadaji. "Pick a category," he said.

Might as well keep it simple, Khadaji thought. "Liquids," he said.

Pen turned back to the computer. "Liquids—give me the total number, please, verbal will do."

"Nineteen thousand three hundred sixty-nine," the computer said.

Khadaji raised his eyebrows. "Buddha! You've made that many different kinds of drinks?"

"So it seems."

"You can't remember them all."

"I probably could, but there wouldn't be much point to it. That's why I have the sphere. Usually, it's enough to learn the ten or twenty most popular ones in any given pub to get by—you can call up anything else if you need it."

Khadaji shook his head again, something he seemed to be doing a lot lately. "I wouldn't have believed there could be that many different kinds of drinks."

Pen chuckled. "People or mues will drink almost anything. Some very strange stuff." He said to the computer, "Liquids—Shin's Kiss, give the ingredient list, visual."

"Running."

Two seconds later, the holoproj lit up with:

SHIN'S KISS

30CC BLENDED LIQUOR - WHISKY STOCK (QUADRANT COMFORT)

30CC FRUIT EXTRACT - COCONUT MILK (ISLE OF WENT)

30CC VEGETABLE EXTRACT - CUCUMBER SOAK (SHIN)

40–45 GRAMS SUCROSE POWDER

DIHYDROGEN OXIDE/CARBON DIOXIDE BLEND, QS TO TOP.

Pen said, "It should be pretty obvious how I have them organized—I go from general to specific, ending with a brand name, if there is one."

"Interesting," Khadaji said. "But it looks pretty tame. I

would think there'd be a lot stranger stuff."

"Don't let the names fool you," Pen said. "Computer, give me an ingredient list of Shin—skip the cucumber."

"Running."

Another list lit the air, this time mostly chemical compounds. Water, ammonia, sodium chloride, potassium chloride, uric acid, creatinine, creatine, urea, phosphorus, magnesium—the list ran on. It didn't mean anything to Khadaji.

"Don't recognize it?" Pen chuckled again. "You should. It's common enough. Urine."

Khadaji blinked. "Piss?"

"Human urine, to be precise. Shin is made by soaking a cucumber in urine for a week, then blending it into a nice frothy texture."

"You're joking."

"Not at all. The drink is quite popular on some worlds—Thompson's Gazelle, for one. They even drank a version of it on Earth at one time, as a remedy for snakebite. And there was one culture which drank the urine of those intoxicated on certain mushrooms—to get the effect without some of the nasty side effects of the mushrooms themselves."

"Shit."

"As I said, there are some strange beings who will drink even stranger drinks." Pen's voice was dry. Khadaji didn't know if he was being had or not. He suspected not.

"There are fewer chemicals used for recreation in the solid and powder categories, fewer still in gases and radiants. And, of course, which ones are legal on which worlds determines their use. Is it a bit more complex than you thought?"

Khadaji stared at the formula for Shin's Kiss, still glowing in the air half a meter away. "Yeah. A bit."

"You don't need a degree on most worlds to challenge

the pubtender's exam, but you do need to learn a few things. We might as well get started."

Khadaji nodded. Well. It wouldn't be dull, not if there were other chemicals like Shin's Kiss. My.

Khadaji had learned a good deal about falling, rolling and tumbling, he realized, as he found himself flying through the air for the tenth time that day. He tucked, hit the grass at a good angle, and came up, without injury or even mild pain.

"You were sleeping," Pen said. He stood three meters away, enveloped in his ever-present shroud. The wind was chilly, it was late fall shading into winter and snow was expected in the mountains within a few days. Khadaji nodded. He hadn't been concentrating and the result showed it. Sumito required total attention for it to work; anything less was cause for instant loss of control. After five local months, he was getting better, but he still had a long way to go. Muscle memory had to be trained, Pen told him, and concentration had to be sharpened to a needle's point. He could walk to the seventy-second step.

As for the planet, he was getting used to it, as well. The smells of the air no longer seemed alien, nor the slight differences in gravity, nor the actinic quality of the local sun's light. The people still waged their war against the Confed, with no success. More troops had been sent to the world and the numbers of the ready-to-die attackers could not overcome the firepower of the Confederation machine. Khadaji wondered sometimes if he and Pen would eventually be the only people alive except troopers. . . .

The snow was piled half a meter thick upon the frozen ground. Khadaji and Pen walked over it on flat, thin sheets of enforced plastic radiating from their slushboots like artificial spider's webs. There was a flaw in the heating system of Khadaji's suit—a spot over his left buttock the size of his hand so cold it was going numb.

"Primary routes of administration?" Pen didn't wear a conditioned suit, only the shroud of his order.

Khadaji's breath made frosty clouds as he spoke. "Oral, anal, vaginal, nasal, ophthalmically, otically, cutaneously." He hit a patch of soft snow with his left web and sank in that direction, almost toppling.

"You forgot poenile—the *meatus urinarius*," Pen said. "Use the mnemonic and you won't."

Khadaji blinked. Damn. The memory device flashed across his mental screen. *On Aqua, crafty people never open virginal orifices.* The first letter of each word stood for one of the primary routes of drug administration.

"Secondary," Pen said.

"Sub-Q, IM, IV, IC."

"Good. We'll do nine kilometers today, so we should have time to cover nasal adequately. Let's start with powders."

Khadaji nodded. It was going to be a long walk.

Khadaji sat nude in the hot swirling waters of the local immersion tub, next to Pen, who was fully clothed in his robes. Nobody seemed to think anything of that, a man dressed to the eyeballs, and Khadaji was quite used to it by now. The thickened water stroked Khadaji's sore muscles and the aroma of mint floated up from the surface with the steam. A plastic roof kept the snow and most of the cold out; it was late, and only a few people enjoyed the water with them.

"What would you get if you served a patron vöremhölts on Primesat?"

Khadaji shifted, to allow the stream of hot water under his left buttock to flow up between his legs. His penis bounced in the stream. "Probably a nice tip," he said. "Vöremhōlts is expensive in the Centauri System."

"And the same drink served on Tatsu would get you . . ."

"Two-to-five in the local prison." Khadaji's voice was dry.

"And on Gebay?"

Khadaji shifted back. The water was causing some blood flow down there he couldn't do anything about now. He looked across the tub at a girl with long white hair. She was young and had a nice smile—not to mention a slim and attractive body he'd noticed when she'd entered the tub. Maybe he could do something about that anatomical swelling. . . .

Pen slapped the water and a glob of it arced up and splashed against Khadaji's face. "Hey!"

"What happens if you serve vöremhōlts on Gebay?"

Khadaji wiped the water from his face. It left a greasy feeling on his skin. "Gebay. Not much. Except in the Konta Compound, where any but church-approved chemicals are illegal. They cut your hair off for selling proscribed drugs. Which doesn't sound all that bad, by the way."

Pen shook his head. "No. They don't cut your body hair. They pull it out, one strand at a time. The pain is supposed to be incredible, after a time, not to mention the anticipation. It takes three days for someone not particularly hirsute— they work straight through, day and night."

Khadaji felt a chill, despite the heat of the water surrounding him. Gebay. The religious compound—serve no vöremhōlts there.

"And the makeup of vöremhōlts?"

"Jahambu bark, majani wormwood and tecal mushrooms, dissolved in a fifty-fifty solution of water and Koji rum."

"And where is the best vöremhōlts made?"

"The Bibi Arusi System—the green moon, Rangi ya majani Mwezi."

Pen nodded; the shroud swirled around him in the water. "Very good," he said. "No more questions for today."

Khadaji inhaled through his nose, enjoying the tickle of the mint. "I have a question," he said. "Will you ever tell me about your order? The Siblings of the Shroud?"

"It is a complex subject," Pen said. "We are called many things: existential humanist/pacifists; elitist intellectual pantheist/positivists; meddling sons-of-bezelworts. A few minutes in a tub would hardly suffice to scratch the surface. Besides, it isn't important for you to know about me, only about yourself. The Shroud isn't your way."

"All right. I have one question you can answer, then. Do you ever take that shroud off?"

Pen laughed. "Certainly. Normally, not in view of another person, that's frowned upon, but when alone, it is allowed. I sleep without it, normally bathe without it, and surely make love without it—in the dark, at least."

Khadaji was surprised about the last. He had somehow thought the order was celibate, though Pen had never said so.

Pen caught Khadaji's look, apparently. He laughed again. "Oh, yes, we have the same stirrings as others. And we indulge them. In fact, I will not be sleeping in our rooms this night."

Khadaji grinned. "Got something lined up?"

Pen said, "I have plans for the evening, yes."

Khadaji's grin widened. Good. He'd have the rooms to himself, and the young woman with hair like snow might also be free. He was thinking of the best way to approach her when Pen stood and waded across the hip-deep tub toward the girl. He extended his arm, dragging the wet folds of the cloth across the scented and thickened water. As Khadaji watched, the girl smiled sweetly and took Pen's hand in her own. Khadaji watched the muscular roll of her buttocks as she and Pen climbed from the tub and walked to the drying rooms. Khadaji found his mouth was agape. He shut it and blinked at the suddenly irritating mint fumes. Well, I'll be damned, he thought. Maybe some of the critics of the Siblings were right. Certainly Pen seemed a son-of-a-bezelwort, at the moment, anyway.

NINE

THEY WENT TO the Beta System, to the fifth planet, called
Rim. As the boxcar dropped from orbit, Khadaji stared out
through the densecris portal. There were patches of smudgy
light against the blackness of the planet's surface, patches
which grew sharper as the boxcar swung its passengers and
cargo closer to the ground.

"Nice view," Khadaji said. "You couldn't get us a daylight arrival so we could see the place, I suppose."

Pen's eyes were closed and he appeared to be sleeping,
but Khadaji knew better. The man never seemed to sleep.
He spoke without opening his eyes. "You didn't bother to
read the history, did you? Didn't even wonder why they call
it 'Darkworld.'"

"I was busy. Studying the tender's exam. Besides, I figured it was probably rock formations or black sands or
something like that."

Pen opened his eyes and glanced out through the densecris plate. "Actually, it's axial tilt and habitable land masses. Most of the people on this world live on a subcontinent which gets daylight only a small portion of each year. It stays somewhere between deep twilight and true night all day in the High Bzer's Glorious State of Khadzharia, for at least twelve of the planet's thirteen months."

Khadaji watched the lights of one city begin to turn into bright, hard diamonds and rubies and sapphires as the boxcar continued its dead-bird descent. "Wonderful place if you're a vampire."

"Or an albino," Pen added.

The old man's name was Kamus and he was the owner of the pub, a long and narrow warren called D. W. Dick's. Khadaji looked around the place carefully, taking it all in. The floor was wood and well-worn, but clean; the tables were small squares with rounded corners, bolted to the floor; the bar itself was antique stressed red plastic, probably almost as shiny as the day it was cast. Behind the bar was a speedex retrieval cabinet for the chem stock, a credit tag reader and comp terminal; on the wall hung a long sword, under a full-size acrylic picture of a nude couple intertwined in apparent passion. Aside from the old man, Pen and Khadaji, the place was empty. It smelled clean.

"We close on Si'days," Kamus said. "Bzer's Decree." He looked carefully at Khadaji. "Your tags say you're qualified, but the patrons in this pub have eclectic tastes. How do you mix a Sinclo Suicide?"

Khadaji wanted to smile, but he kept his face impassive. "Twenty-five cc's each gin, scotch, amberglow and Spandle yeast, in a tall glass of Bern's champagne."

The old man nodded. A lock of white hair fell across his forehead. "A Scarlet Dream?"

"Grind five grams of red coke into a fine powder and mix with one half gram of verisol—any inhaler will do, but it's best in a number six Marietta."

Kamus nodded again. "One more. Bloody Mary?"

Khadaji allowed himself the grin, this time. That was an old one, Pen had made him learn it early on. It was perfect for curing the aftereffects of alcohol intoxicaton. "Forty-five cc's vodka, ninety cc's tomato juice, one cc Worcestershire sauce, two cc's Tabasco, trace pepper, lemon slice, one dissolved tab AA-complex. Mix cold with cracked ice and strain into a frosted glass."

The owner of the pub returned Khadaji's smile, then looked at Pen. "Seems to know his stuff. Your rec?"

Pen nodded. "Vouch and backup."

Kamus sucked at his teeth. "All right. You're hired. Corpse-stealer's shift, basic-and-half—divvy with the floor. When can you start?"

Khadaji was startled. He understood about half of what the old man had just said. Before he could speak, Pen said, "Fine. He can start tonight. Where can we get rooms?"

"Wait, hold it a—" Khadaji began.

"Quiet," Pen ordered. "The rooms?"

The old man grinned and wheezed a little and told Pen where they could find rooms.

As they walked out into the warm darkness, Khadaji started asking his questions. "Corpse-stealer's shift?"

"Midnight until dawn, twelve hundred to oh-six hundred. In the early days on this world, people used to bury the dead."

Khadaji shook his head. "Like on old Earth. I never understood why—such a waste of raw material. And basic-and-half, divvy with the floor? What are we talking about?"

"Minimum stads to start, but you get a percentage of gratuities left by patrons, usually divided equally among the workers on any shift."

"Vouch and backup?"

"A long time ago, I worked for the previous owner of

the place. I—ah—developed a good reputation. If I'm willing to vouch for you, it's a point in your favor. Backup means I'll cover for you if you have to miss a shift for some reason."

"That might be rough on you," Khadaji said. "Having to work my shift and yours."

Pen stopped and smiled; the movement was invisible through the folds of his costume, but Khadaji knew. "Did you hear me say anything about me working? You support us for awhile, Emile; I've got meditation to catch up on."

Khadaji thought about that for a moment. Well. It was only fair; after all, Penn had been carrying the cargo since they'd met.

Pen came with him the first night and stood in the background as Kamus introduced Khadaji to the others on the shift. Even with the dampers on, it was noisy, there were a couple of hundred people packed into the place. He yelled at Banrose, the headserver, managed a smile across the bar at Shandu and Gretyl, two more servers, and got a frosty nod from Mang, the "crowd control officer."

Kamus said, "That's pretty much the crew, except for Juete—she's late, as usual. Hop on back there and work with Lu Shan for a few minutes, get the hang of the layout."

Khadaji glanced at Pen, who stood nearby, watching the crowd, then nodded at Kamus. "Sir," he said.

"None of that," Kamus said, smiling. "Last time somebody called me 'sir' I had to duck to keep him from shooting me. Call me Kamus."

Khadaji nodded and headed for the bar. He took a deep-breath and let it out slowly. The battle on Maro, with its sense of cosmic consciousness, was still firmly embedded in his mind, but he had to believe Pen's advice—he had to start somewhere. Pubtender Khadaji. Well. It had an interesting ring, at least.

• • •

Khadaji was busy. He supposed it would get easier as he learned the systems, the locations of various chems, the ways to mix common ones faster, but for the moment, he was running at full throttle, jets flaming, trying to keep up with the demand. The standard single-ingredient chems were easy, just a quick tab touch and the computer would dispense those automatically. But some of the patrons were as odd as Pen had first told him. He was bent over a concoction called Hen's Teeth when a soft and deep female voice said, "I need four splashes, a Wizard's Ring and a double fire brandy."

Khadaji looked up, mildly irritated with the server.

Later, he would swear his heart had stopped and his vocal cords had been suddenly paralyzed. The most beautiful creature he had ever seen stood there. She had encountered his reaction before, it seemed, for she smiled slightly and said, "I'm Juete. You must be the new tender."

Khadaji managed a blink, but no words. Shoe-et-tay, she called herself. Wonderful. Amazing. She stood a hair over a hundred and sixty centimeters high, weighed maybe fifty-five kilos, and had smooth white skin, white hair to her buttocks, and pink eyes. He wasn't sure about the last, the lights were dim, but she was as clear an albino as he'd ever seen. She wore a jet body stocking which was nearly as revealing as full nudity, though it covered her from neck to toes. Against the black of the sheer cloth, her face and hands seemed to shine with pure whiteness.

"My drinks?"

Khadaji fumbled the drink he was building, managed to set the glass down without spilling more than half of it, and hurried to fill her order. Somehow, he managed it. Then she was gone. He stared after her, feeling stupid, feeling as he had just before the first time he had ever made love to a girl.

Kamus cackled behind him. Khadaji turned.

"Never saw an exotic before, that's plain enough."

Khadaji snapped himself out of his daze and hurried to rework the Hen's Teeth. The old man hovered next to him. "Genetic restructuring," he said. "Somebody figured since it was dark all the time, albinos would feel right at home. It was before the Chromosome Charter and the genetic laws, but they tend to breed true."

Khadaji tried to say something. "She's—I—it—uh. . . ."

The old man cackled again, trailing off into a wheeze and cough. When he could breathe again, he said, "Yeah, I understand, son. That's why I don't term her for coming in late, she is good for business." He laughed again, then wandered off. As he passed the sword hanging under the acrylic picture, he paused to stroke the handle.

By the time Juete had returned for her twentieth order, Khadaji was able to relax enough to speak and pretend to a kind of normalcy. He hoped.

But the conversations were limited to drinks and powders; both the server and tender were too busy to stop and chat. Khadaji found it was hard for him to judge her age. At first, he had thought she was very young, she seemed barely past puberty for a standard human female, on looks alone. But she moved too well, her timing and pacing were obviously well-practiced, a thing which only came with age. Such a joy to watch move, she was, ah—

He shook his head. He was a young man, but hardly a virginal wheatseed fresh off an agropod; he had spent six years in the military, had been many sexual places with more than a few people. Why was this woman so—so—so . . . whatever it was she was? He felt smitten—and foolish for feeling that way.

The morning worked its way by without any major disasters on his part. Oh, he did flub a few orders, managed to put bitter tair in a drink supposed to be sweet, but all in all, it went well. He was tired, but pleased. And smitten, of course. At six hundred, the relief crew began to filter into the pub. When the dayshift tender arrived, Khadaji tried to find the girl, but Juete was gone.

Pen seemed to materialize from the smoke-filled room, to stand next to Khadaji. Before he could speak, his teacher said one word: "Pheromones."

"Excuse me?"

"The female exotic. She produces concentrated and enhanced sexual-chemical signals, specific for human males. Part of the original genetic programming built into her ancestors' systems. They were designed as sexual toys, you know."

Khadaji swallowed and shook his head. "No. I didn't know."

"You found her attractive. Unusually so."

"Yeah." He recalled the feeling. Knowing why the woman drew him seemed to make no difference. It was that gut-level versus intellectual-level thing again. The brain might know, but the gut felt. And, in this case, it was a portion of his anatomy somewhat lower than his gut which seemed to control his interest in the exotic girl he'd just met.

Pen said nothing, only stood there amid the flick-smoke and stale odors of human bodies and chem, waiting.

Finally, Khadaji said, "Let's go to the rooms. I'm a little tired."

The routine was established. Days, Pen schooled Khadaji in martial techniques. Nights, they slept—at least Khadaji did. Early mornings, there was the pub. After a few weeks, Khadaji had the hang of it. He got to know Banrose and Shandu and Gretyl, the servers; managed a passing relationship with Mang, the bouncer, and listened to the old man Kamus spin adventure stories in the early hours at the pub. But Juete, the exotic, seemed to be avoiding him, save for orders at the bar. Aside from that, Khadaji was comfortable with the new routine. Too comfortable, he thought. Something was bound to happen to screw things up. At four hundred on a slow W'nday, something did.

Kamus was near the starboard end of the bar, leaning on the thick plastic, telling one of his fantasies to a group of old men like himself. The Dick—as it was called by almost everybody—was nearly empty, only a dozen or so of the night people quietly smoking or drinking. The vampire crowd, Khadaji thought of them, they came out after midnight.

"—giant spider," Kamus said, "damned near the size of a big dog. Well, I have to admit I was a touch worried—"

Khadaji stirred a cocktail and blasted the finished drink with a spray of liquid nitrogen, freezing the fluid into a slush. He dropped a cherry onto it and turned toward his next drink. At a table near the port side of the bar, three men seemed to be raising their voices a bit louder than the usual background din, but not enough to blank Kamus.

"—skewered that fucker on my blade, but he kept wiggling and reaching for me—"

Add carbon dioxide for the bubbles, now—what was the last? Ah, yes, the still wine—

The voices of the three men increased in volume. They were arguing about something. Juete was their server and she seemed somehow involved in the discussion. Khadaji saw Mang begin to edge in the direction of the table.

"—green blood, it had! Copper-based, I think, but it was damned well bleeding all over me and my sword—"

Khadaji was reaching for a mixer when he heard the *whump!* of a compressed gas gun. It was a sound he'd heard enough during the Kontrau'lega Break. He ducked reflexively and swept his gaze around the room.

One of the three arguing men stood by the table, pointing

a long-barreled air pistol at the downed form of a second man. As Khadaji watched, the man with the pistol took deliberate aim at the fallen man's head and fired again. Khadaji heard both the *whump!* of the gun and the wet thump of the steel projectile as it smacked into the man's skull.

Mang jumped toward the killer, his hand digging for his own weapon. Before he could clear his stunner, the third man kicked his chair away and pointed a hand wand at the charging bouncer. He fired, and the pulse flared out, flashing Mang and the two customers who had jumped up at the first shot. Two more patrons reeled away with peripheral shock.

The whole sequence had taken maybe five seconds.

Khadaji took it all in. There was no point in becoming a dead hero, he decided. If they pointed their weapons in his direction, he would duck behind the bar, otherwise, he wasn't planning on moving and drawing their attention.

Then the man with the air pistol grinned widely and pointed the weapon at Juete. "Your time is come, twat."

Khadaji went cold. Without pausing, he vaulted the bar, hit the floor, and took two running steps. He reached out, clamped his hands onto the air pistol and twisted, swinging his arms in a hard half-circle in front of his face. The torque snapped the gunman from his feet; Khadaji heard the man's wrist break as the pistol clattered onto the wooden floor. All of Pen's training seemed to focus as Khadaji kicked the pistol away and watched the killer fall. Khadaji was in control, he knew just what he had to do. He turned to face the second man, who was also trying to turn and bring the hand wand to bear. He didn't need to be accurate, the pulse was much like a shot sprayer, and he was almost there—

Khadaji saw the flash of bright steel, a blur in the dim light—

The hand holding the wand jerked away from the rest of the man's arm and fell with a clump and clatter. The man screamed and clutched his bloody wrist with his other hand.

He went pale and collapsed, the red pumping from the stump
with each pulse. Khadaji looked away from the bleeding
man to see Kamus holding a sword with both wrinkled and
knobby hands. For a second, the younger man could see
what the older must have been like many years past, the
fire was dimmer now, but still there.

"Get the medics," Kamus said.

Somebody ran for the com.

Gretyl found a pressure patch and managed to fit it to
the severed wrist, to stop the bleeding.

"Save the hand," Kamus ordered. "Stick it in a foam bag
and put in the cooler for the medics."

Khadaji was feeling ill. The adrenalin in him was ebbing
and he felt tired, afraid, and shaky. It was a reaction he'd
felt after battles, he knew it would pass, but the desire to
run and hide was strong.

Someone touched his shoulder. Juete. "Thank you," she
said. "He was going to kill me."

Despite a feeling of nausea and his jittery hands, Khadaji
felt a strong desire for the exotic, he wanted to grab her,
to kiss her, to tear the thin body stocking away and feel her
naked against him. Was it the violence? Or were her pheromones raging from her own fear, singing to him? He managed a short nod. "No problem," he said. "You know them?"

"I used to work for him." She glanced at the man with
the broken wrist. "He was my . . . agent."

Khadaji nodded again. He didn't ask what kind of work
she had done for a man who had just killed another. He
wasn't sure he wanted to know.

Juete reached up to touch Khadaji's arm, just above the
elbow. Her fingers were warm even through the shirt he
wore. "You took a great risk for me." Her voice was soft,
deep and it seemed to draw at something in his core.

"Well. I can't have people shooting my servers, can I?"
It sounded inept and foolish even as he said it, but it broke

the tension. Juete laughed, and Khadaji with her. She smiled at him, her hand still touching his arm. "Yes. There is more to you than you would reveal, I can sense that. Perhaps we can talk later?"

Khadaji's mouth was full of glue, his tongue was made of lead, his throat constricted with plastcrete; he couldn't even nod this time. But she could see it in his face, and she smiled again.

"Fun's over, people," Kamus said. "Suppose we clean up and get back to work." He prodded the man with the broken wrist with the tip of the sword and the man stood and walked toward the bar. In a few moments, the medics and nabs arrived to haul away the dead and injured. Mang would survive, but he would be out of action for a month, the other customers would live, as well. Only the man Juete's "agent" had killed was beyond help, and that because of the brain injury. Kamus's sword hadn't damaged the wrist or hand of the wandslinger too badly, the limb would be reconnected easily enough. But despite the deaths and injuries, Khadaji counted the affair as a plus. Juete had smiled at him, had touched him.

The rest of the shift passed in a kind of limbo. Khadaji mixed the drinks automatically, while Kamus polished the blood from his sword, occasionally laughing to himself softly as he wiped the mirror steel.

TEN _____

PEN SHOWED HIM the knife before they went outside. Khadaji hefted the weapon, made a few slashes in the air, then stared at the blade. "It looks like a banana," he said.

Pen nodded. "It's based on the shape of a tooth, actually. In the southern part of the subcontinent there used to be a saber-toothed carnivore, a large cat-like beast. It had a set of slashing tusks on the sides of its mouth, four of them, pointing down."

Khadaji had learned to pay attention to the next question any such statement by Pen invariably brought up. So he asked it. "Why would a creature evolve such natural weaponry, I wonder?"

"Roots," Pen said. Khadaji thought he detected a pleased note in his voice. "The southern region is rocky and full of caves. A lot of wildlife used to inhabit the caves, and that's where the predator did its hunting. There is a kind of plant which traps its victims in a sticky root system and then drains the fluids from the body. The tusks seemed to have evolved for slashing the roots."

"Interesting. And efficient."

"Not in the long run," Pen said. "The plants are still there, they are very tenacious. Men have put the predators down."

Khadaji glanced at the knife. The handle was of some dark and close-grained wood; there was a brass cap where it met the curved steel, which was sharp on the inner edge of the curve; the back of the blade had a notched, serrated pattern near the handle. Holding the knife with the point toward the floor, it was easy to imagine it being the tooth of some meat-eating creature.

"There is a lot of mining done in that region," Pen continued. "The saber-tooth knives were popular among the miners in the early days of men on this world. Hand-burners sometimes flamed out or had power packs go dead. A knife was more dependable."

Khadaji got the distinct impression Pen was trying to make some point, but he wasn't certain just what it was. "Seems to me it would be easier to avoid the roots," he said.

"Ah, but that's the trick. The things grew incredibly fast, were resistant to most herbicides, and had a trick of hugging the roof or walls of a cave or tunnel, of blending into the surface so they were difficult to see. Then, when an animal—or man—moved past, they were triggered."

When did he learn all this? "I see."

"Yes. Sometimes trouble cannot be avoided. And in some cases, the most simple preparations are the wisest."

Pen extended his hand and Khadaji passed the knife to him. "Shall we?" Pen turned toward the door of their cubicle. Khadaji followed him outside.

It was dark, of course. One of the planet's two moons was visible, and there were thousands of stars in the galaxy's edge to the clump of the Whore's Pubes. It was warm and humid and insects buzzed drowsily in air which smelled faintly of wood smoke. The two men walked to a clear patch under a circle of low-sode light cast by the yard lamp.

Pen turned and faced Khadaji. The man in the gray shroud seemed relaxed, there was no special stance to mark his intent. The curved knife was held low, by his right leg, invisible. Khadaji knew it was there, just as he knew what his teacher was about to do with—

Pen . . . shifted. He didn't lunge or leap or fly; he simply moved, somehow scooting across the two meters which separated them; it was incredibly fast. He snapped the knife up, edge leading sickle-like, the point aimed at Khadaji's scrotum. If it connected it would gut him from groin to sternum, Khadaji knew.

Khadaji stepped aside. There was no jerkiness in his movement, it was an unhurried shift much like Pen's own motion.

Pen converted the upward slash into a loop across his body and out to his side, a backhand for Khadaji's throat.

Khadaji ducked and the knife cut only air over his head. He slid back another step, anticipating Pen's next strike.

Pen continued his circular motion, whipping the knife over and down, so it would have buried its point in the top of Khadaji's skull—had he not moved.

Pen stepped back a meter and faced Khadaji. He brought the knife behind his back, out of sight. "Ah. So your encounter last night in the pub has changed you."

Khadaji smiled. "Those men would have killed me."

"And if you fail to move, I won't?" Pen edged closer. "You think I would pull my strike?"

"No. But you don't want me to die. If you hit me, I think you would drop the knife and do your best to keep me alive."

"You think so? If my sumito teaching is a failure, why

would you be worth keeping alive?" He moved, and the knife became a blur as he slashed, a figure-eight criss-cross.

Khadaji backed up easily, staying just out of range. He said, "There's a difference. It's hard to explain. I feel the energy—you're a teacher—they were killers."

Pen laughed. "Were you afraid of them?"

"Yes. More after it was over."

"Good. But you didn't let your fear paralyze you."

Khadaji shifted a hair to his left, ready for Pen's next attack. "There's something else," he said. "I was afraid, but I was also a lot more alive. And I was . . . worried."

Pen made another pass, slicing the warm darkness with the knife based on the tooth of a long-dead predator. Khadaji moved from his path; this time, he snapped his own hand up, the edge leading, and chopped at Pen's wrist. Pen managed to pull his hand back, twisting the knife to cut, but both attacks missed. "Good," Pen said. "You were worried, you said. About the exotic?"

"Yes."

Pen spun in toward Khadaji, the knife whirling like a rotor blade. Khadaji dropped to the ground and rolled to the side, then back up, out of range. He tried a sweep with his right leg, but Pen jumped over his foot and stabbed at his face. This time, Khadaji's block connected solidly and knocked the hand with the weapon away. Pen switched the knife to his opposite hand.

"I'm not one to give advice on such things," Pen said. "We of the Shroud tend to believe in teaching those things we know we can teach, and in affairs of the heart—or gonads—there are no real experts. Love, like zen, cannot be learned, only felt."

Khadaji thought about that for a moment as Pen circled to his left, holding the knife loosely. "But you have an opinion about her."

Pen shrugged. "What I think isn't important. What you

think is, in this case. I have been on the Disk for what seems a long time; one passes the same point more than once, even though it is usually at an upward or downward spiral."

Again, Pen moved, the knife leading.

Again, Khadaji shifted away from the killing blade. He tried to trip his teacher as he passed, but missed.

"Is that why you don't tell me about the Shroud?" Khadaji asked. "Do you feel as if it's something which can't be taught?"

"Hardly. It's just that your circuit lies in another plane. You'll never be a priest, Emile. You will be a great man, in your own way. Eventually."

There came another attack. Even as he moved, Khadaji saw the end of this series. He knew he was in perfect balance, in total control of himself. Since Pen was attacking, he had that small disadvantage of the attacker, despite his own years of sumito practice. An attacker must reach beyond himself; a defender did not need to; this gave the edge to a defender, assuming equal skill otherwise.

Pen cut downward with the root knife; Khadaji pivoted and flipped the heel of his right hand into Pen's shoulder, at the same time he caught Pen's left wrist with his own left hand. Khadaji twisted, and the knife spun from Pen's grip, falling in a lazy twirl to stick in the bare ground. Khadaji continued the movement, levering Pen past him as he dropped to one knee. Pen stumbled as Khadaji released his grip, then dived into a perfect roll, an egg rather than a ball. He came up and stepped around casually to face Khadaji. "Very good," he said. "Excellent."

Khadaji grinned. It was the first time since they'd begun training, almost a year now, that he'd ever thrown Pen. He was both pleased and proud. Although there was a small voice in the back of his mind which wondered if maybe the old man hadn't allowed it, for reasons of his own.

The dim lights reflected in the bright red plastic of the bar's surface gave her face a rosy glow as she smiled at him. "Would you like to have breakfast with me after the shift ends?"

"Yes," he said, feeling his heart pound faster. "I'd like that very much."

"Good. I have some stuffed Mikkel leaves a friend brought back from the bright belt, I'll cook them for us."

Khadaji swallowed dryness as he watched her walk away carrying her tray of chem. Breakfast. In her cube. Alone. He felt the beginnings of an erection stir, and he quickly turned back to his next order. *She only asked you to have breakfast with her, fool, nothing more. That's all.* But he spilled half a bottle of wine as he visualized her stripping the body stocking away. It would never happen, he thought.

She had black silk sheets on her bed and the contrast between them and her naked skin was incredible. His own brown arm looked somehow alien as he reached across her breasts to squeeze her shoulder. He pulled her against him, kissing her softly. Her lips flowered and parted and her tongue slowly slid along the sides of his own tongue. "Ummm." Her voice was a small moan. He leaned back, breaking the kiss, and looked at her. Definitely pink eyes. And pink nipples, budded up like tiny hard roses now. Perfectly white pubic hair, as fine and downy as that on a baby's head. Her body was slender and taut, the muscles firm as she moved back against him. He slid his hand down her back and over one buttock, marvelling at the smoothness of her perfect too-pale skin. He moved his hand around over her hip, feeling the padded sharpness of the bone pointing at him. She lifted her leg and pointed her toes at the ceiling, opening up for him. Her vaginal lips were delicate, hot and slick, and she moaned again as he traced them, first the outer, then the inner. She shuddered as he touched her clitoris, and dug her fingers into the hard muscles of his back. He slid down, then, to taste her there, to smell the musk of her as he softly waggled his tongue back and forth, following the path his fingers had taken a moment before, tasting and probing gently, then deeper, nibbling at her lips with his own.

"Oh, gods," she said. "Yes!"

He lifted her legs with his hands, pushing her knees back, raising her higher and wider. He stabbed deeper with his tongue. She began to move against his mouth, in that oldest of rhythms. She came hard, he could feel the pulse around his tongue, against his lips, and he grinned. He flicked his tongue back and forth a few more times.

She tangled her hands in his hair and pulled his face away. "Easy. Let me catch my breath before you do any more of that."

"No problem," he said.

She moved suddenly, sliding across the jet silk, turning and taking his penis into her mouth in a single, smooth motion. He felt her lips touch the base as she took the length of him into her throat. Damn! She moved, and he felt like a boy again, so hard he was afraid his organ would burst. All the learned techniques with all the partners over all the years meant nothing, his control was completely gone. When she found the base of his prosate with her finger and pressed, he felt as if a dam had burst within his groin. Oh, God!

When he stopped throbbing, she pulled away slowly, flicking the tip of his still-hard penis with her tongue.

She turned around to snuggle next to him.

"Now I know what an avalanche must feel like," he said.

"It was pretty good, wasn't it?" She smiled at him.

Khadaji propped himself up on one elbow. She was the most beautiful woman he had ever seen, he was sure of that. And she seemed to exude sexual attraction, more now

than before the shattering climax she'd just given him. He
reached for her and hugged her to him, sliding into her as
she rolled onto her back and clasped his buttocks with both
hands. She was tight, but lubricated, and they fit together
as if they had been custom-designed for each other. The
dance became frantic, as they pounded each other faster and
faster. "I—love—you," he said, his voice keeping time
with his thrusts. But the words were lost in the storm.

Pen was sitting quietly in the center of his bed, his eyes
closed, when Khadaji came into the room. It was late, only
a couple of hours before Khadaji's shift was to begin and
he was tired. Though hardly unhappy.

Pen said, "And . . . ?"

There was no need to say more. They had developed a
feel for each other's mood, at times. "She is wonderful,"
Khadaji said. "I love her."

Pen nodded, but said nothing. There was a long pause.

"I can't explain it," Khadaji began. "She—"

"There is no need to explain. I understand. The time was
approaching and now it is here."

Somehow, that sounded ominous. "The time?"

"For me to continue upon my circuit. And you on yours."

Khadaji was stunned. "What?"

Pen smiled. "You will want to be with your beloved.
You have things to learn from her."

"But—but—that doesn't mean—"

"Ah, but it does," Pen said, his voice soft. He unfolded
his legs from the meditation knot and shifted to the edge of
the bed, then stood. He faced Khadaji, still smiling. "You've
learned what I can teach you. What you need now is new
teachers, and time. Experience will fill in many of the gaps."

Khadaji stared at the robed figure, still feeling shocked.
Sure, he'd said in the beginning it was only temporary, but,
this wasn't right. It was Juete, she was the crux, that was

why he was leaving. He thought about her, and about Pen, who had been father-brother-teacher since they'd met. In that moment, Khadaji knew, he *knew* that if he offered to forget her, Pen would stay. This was some kind of test. He thought again about Juete, about the day they had spent together, only leaving the bed long enough to pee or get a drink, about the passion he'd felt, he still felt for her. Was it any more than lust? Did he love her, as he'd said? Yes, he was sure he did. Could he give her up, to keep Pen? But if he was planning to leave anyway, it would be a wasted gesture to even offer, wouldn't it? He remembered her hands and mouth, touching him. Pen was going anyhow, Juete was only making it happen a few days or weeks sooner. Khadaji told himself it wasn't a rationalization on his part, but far back in his mind, a little voice laughed malevolently.

Juete smiled at him across the red bar and Khadaji reflexively smiled back. He watched her walk away and felt desire for her even as he felt disgusted with himself. Was he doing as so many others in the military had done? Was he thinking with his dick?

He shook his head and wiped at a spill on the bar. No. He loved the exotic woman, there was more to her than sex. She was intriguing, there was a depth to her, she was . . . exotic, in the truest sense of that word. But Pen—

Pen was gone. Khadaji had seen him off at the sling. Pen hadn't seemed disturbed or sad at going. He had laughed, he had hugged Khadaji, he had told him not to worry. Things would be fine, in the end, he was destined for what he was destined for—who could say where the Disk would spin him?

As Pen waited for the boxcar to helix, he reached within the folds of his robe and came out with a small steel marble in his hand. He extended it to Khadaji.

"What's this?" Khadaji said, as he took the marble.

"My compendia. The works of my career in tending pub."

"I can't take—"

"I have copies, Emile."

"You've given me so much already."

"Only what I could, little enough. Someday, when you are where you will be, I will smile and wish it were more."

Khadaji felt a lance of guilt. "You don't have to go, Pen."

"I do, Emile, but there is one more thing I would like to do before I leave." With that, Pen reached up within his hood and pulled the cross-scarf covering his face away. For the first time, Khadaji saw the features of the man who had lived with him for over a year. Slowly, Pen leaned forward; slowly, he pressed his lips against Khadaji's lips, and kissed him. Then, the scarf was back. None of the few passengers waiting for the boxcar had seen Pen's naked face, no one save Khadaji. His tears ran freely as Pen entered the boxcar and was slung out of Khadaji's life.

ELEVEN

THE ROUTINE IN the pub settled into a comfortable rhythm. Once in a while, somebody would ask for some unusual drink or powder, even a radiant. Kamus would walk by and smile and pause to stroke the old sword hanging on the wall. He seemed pleased with Khadaji's work. Pen was gone, but Khadaji still practiced the self-control forms, the dances of sumito, alone. It was as Pen had said, an opponent wasn't needed if you could control your own actions precisely enough. And there was Juete. He had little time for anything else.

Juete was incredible. She could drain him as no other woman had ever drained him. Sometimes they made love until he could barely remember who he was, sunk into a satisfied stupor with a stupid grin locked into place.

He also learned about her in other ways. One morning, after a quiet lovemaking session, she lay on the bed, cradling his head in the crook of her arm, petting his face with her fingertips. "Such a sweet boy," she said.

"Boy?"

She smiled down at him. "It's all relative, lover. I might not be old enough to be your mother, but I certainly could be your big sister."

"Only if I were incestuous," he said.

"There are worse things. But I do have a few standard years on you."

He'd suspected as much, but merely said, "So?"

She seemed to stare through the bedroom walls. The smell of sex hung in the air, fighting a losing battle with the stick of incense she'd thumbed into life earlier. Sandalwood, he thought. Or maybe some kind of musk. Finally, she said, "Older doesn't necessarily mean wiser, Emile, but it does mean older. More . . . experienced. More adept at dealing with the galaxy, at . . . taking care of oneself."

Her tone was disturbing, and he wanted to lighten the mood. "Well, I'm not exactly freshly minted, you know. I understand a few things." He tried to laugh, but it fell flat.

She bent to kiss him, first on the forehead, then on his closed eyelids. She didn't have to say it aloud; what he heard silently was, *No, you don't understand, Emile.*

During a lull late in his shift, Khadaji listened to old man Kamus finish one of his tales for a few of the regulars. Juete had left early, since things were slow and she said she was tired. When Kamus finished his story, and the small gathering began to break up, the old man turned to talk to his pubtender. "You seem to be working out okay," he said. "You've been good for business."

Khadaji was pleased, but said, "I'm just doing what you pay me for, Kamus."

"Yeah, but you get along well with the customers, they like you, and now that you and Juete are living together, things have been a lot quieter during corpse-stealer's shift."

Khadaji didn't understand. "Quieter?"

The old man drew himself a mug of splash and took a big swallow of the liquid. He leaned back against the bar. "Sure. You don't understand about exotics, son, even though you're pretty tight with one. They cause trouble among regular people."

Khadaji felt himself stiffen; he tried to relax, using one of Pen's mantras. The old man caught it, though.

"Don't take it personal, son. Juete is a fine woman, but she can't help being an exotic. It's the same for all of them, men or women, old or young. They attract basic stock humans like shit does flies, something chemical, I think."

Khadaji remembered Pen's comment about pheromones. But that didn't matter—

"Anyway, there are people who get real possessive. You know a lot of exotics work as prostitutes?"

Khadaji nodded. Juete had told him.

"A lot of them don't want to, but it's kind of what they were bred for, originally. Usually, you see an exotic, you see a collection of people clustered around 'em, trying to figure a way to get some kind of piece of them."

Khadaji said nothing, but he wondered what the old man was getting at.

"Yo, Emile, slide me another stinger down here, would you?" Khadaji looked up and smiled at the short man sitting at the end of the bar. He built the drink, while Kamus kept talking.

"Normally, people around here know not to start trouble in the Dick." He glanced at the sword on the wall. "I don't much care for it and people know it. Even so, some nights I've had to have Mang toss guys—and women—with their tongues hanging out over Juete through the door. After you jumped the cuntmaster and his cur, word got out you were fast and dangerous. So people are even more careful than usual trying to get to Juete. In here, at least."

Something about the way he said it made Khadaji's gut freeze, as though someone had stuck him with a shard of dry ice. *In here?* What did he mean by that? And *cunt-master?*

Kamus wandered off, to talk to a pair of old women who had just come into the pub, and Khadaji didn't have a chance to ask about his comments. He wasn't sure he would have asked even if the old boy had stuck around.

When he got to her cube, Juete was waiting for him. She stood naked in the doorway, and any doubts or fears he might have felt were erased by the sight of her dropping to her knees to untab the fastener of his pants, and by the feathery touch of her lips on his hard flesh.

People talked to him at the bar, as Pen said they would. He listened with half his attention as he worked, and the conversations tended to run together. A lot of what was said was supposed to be unique, and each person seemed to think it was, but it wasn't long before he'd heard a lot of stories with common threads running through them.

"—me, said I couldn't do the fucking work—can you believe that? So I told him, 'Listen, tarpsucker, I been here twenty-two standard years, before you were finished fresher-training, and I know my fucking job better than you do! If you don't like it, you take it to the steward,' I said, 'and fuck you'—"

"—younger and tighter, that's all he wants! Buddha, I had the goddamn surgery like he wanted, I took the rejuve to the limit, I don't look sixty, I look thirty-five, see how they still stand up? And I know the tricks, buddy, believe it, I can make a man howl like a dog, if I want, and shit, he's off sticking it to some teenpuss young enough to be our granddaughter! She can't know anything! Why? I don't understand men, they're such assholes—"

"—failed the exam, flat, I sucked it, I'm cold meat in the eyes of parents and sibs and classies, I am *raised,* you bury? Sure, they give you a second blast, but you have to wait six months, and that'll be during the Light—nobody will want to play stroke-the-grad in the sunshine—!"

Khadaji gave advice. He nodded a lot, made sympathetic murmurs, and so a lot of the customers thought he knew more than he did. But he was learning. The lot of man was made up of lots of individuals, and the stories rang true, if similar. Love, hate, lust, fear, the emotions were the same. And there was another emotion he found, too. . . .

The man was a freight handler, off a freighter dropping heavy machinery on planet from out-system. He was big, well built and attractive. He sat at the bar, wearing a coverall spotted with dirt and machine lube, sniffing spirals of kick-dust and laughing. He was talking to a local next to him.

"—best I ever had. I've had 'em on twelve worlds in four systems, but this pussy was *talented!* I never had an exotic before and they are everything they're cracked up to be!" He laughed at his own pun, and shook his head. "She couldn't get enough, she turned me every which way but loose. I wished I had a gallon of android, I would have wore myself down to a nub. And she didn't charge me a demi-stad, either. The best I ever had and it was *free!* Shit, I might just jump ship and stay here—" he stopped talking and stared at someone in the pub. Then the freight handler nudged the local with one beefy hand and said, "Shit, there she is now!"

Khadaji turned, to see who had made the man so happy.

And found himself looking at Juete.

It had to be a mistake. Even as he thought it, he knew

it wasn't—Juete wasn't somebody you could forget. Then he thought, it must have happened before they'd met; Juete's past was her own, he couldn't fault her for that—

The big man slid from the barstool, grinning. "It's been two days, I'm ready for another round," he said.

Two days. Khadaji felt that lance of dry ice again, only this time it ran from his bowels to his brain, turning him numb. He watched, detached, as the freight handler approached Juete. Two days ago, she had left early, had been gone for hours before he'd gone to meet her. But it couldn't be.

The look Juete gave the man was not that of someone meeting a stranger. She smiled and said something—Khadaji was too far away to hear what—and the man smiled back at her. Khadaji turned away and stared at the wall, not seeing it.

It was an irrational feeling, he knew. Monofidelity was an archaic concept, one he'd never believed in before. People did not own each other in a civilized society; no one had the right to expect another to become any sort of chattel. Certainly he had enjoyed a liberal intercourse all his life, and there was no reason to expect Juete had done differently. *Cuntmaster* came to his mind, a word he had refused to speculate upon after Kamus had dropped it into their conversation a couple of days earlier. No, her past was her own, just as her present and future should also be. Khadaji knew that. Intellectually, he knew.

Why, then, did he feel like screaming? Was he like all the others who hung around the exotics? Possessive? Jealous?

"Not now!" That was Juete's voice, pitched to carry.

Khadaji turned, to see the big freight handler holding onto the exotic's arm, urging her in the direction of the front exit. She looked at Khadaji, her eyes pleading.

He didn't remember the move, but he was suddenly on

the outside of the bar, heading for them. His mind was filled
with murder. He would chop the freight handler into bloody
slabs—

Kamus moved to block his path. "Easy, son. Mang's got
it."

Khadaji faltered for a step. He was about to tell the old
man to get the hell out of his way, but he saw the bouncer
holding the freight handler's arm as he had held Juete's,
walking him toward the exit.

Khadaji's rage bubbled, heading toward a full boil. No.
He didn't want Mang to walk the man out! He wanted to
handle it himself. She was his woman! He wanted to—
to—

To what, Khadaji? said the little voice that lived deep in
his mind. *To kill him? Like you did the fanatics on Maro?
Is that the mark of a civilized society? When you grow angry,
solve the problem with death?*

He stopped breathing for a moment with the shock of
what he had been about to do. The old man stood his ground,
watching, and Khadaji's hatred and anger left him in a rush
as he exhaled. There was something very wrong with what
he'd been about to do, something which was linked to the
way the Confed squatted upon the worlds and systems of
the galaxy. It was important, but he couldn't quite grasp it,
it eluded him.

"You okay, son?"

He wasn't, but Khadaji nodded.

Juete walked to where the two men stood. Kamus looked
at the two of them for a moment, then left.

"He was your lover," Khadaji said. The anger was gone,
but the gut-twist of jealousy was still there.

"Yes. Briefly."

"Two days ago. When you left work early."

"Yes."

"There have been others since we—"

"Yes."

Khadaji turned his head and looked away from her. Behind the bar, Kamus was mixing some chem, doing Khadaji's job. What customers there were paid no attention to the couple standing and talking.

"It bothers you," she said. "That's why I didn't tell you."

"But—why? Aren't I enough for you?"

He did not expect the answer she gave. "No. You aren't."

It hurt, to hear that. He wanted to hit her, but instead, he clenched his hands into fists. He felt the nails cut into his palms. There was a wrongness here—

"It isn't your fault," she said, her voice soft. "It's the way we are. What attracts you to me works both ways, Emile. My drives are more intense than yours—or any normal human's. I must have that energy, it's built into me the same way as the color of my hair and eyes are built in."

Khadaji did not speak, he only stared at her.

"I *like* it, Emile. Sex. The entire process, meeting someone new, the discovery, the consummation, the afterglow."

"But I *love* you," he said. It sounded like a whine, even as he said it.

"I know. And I love you. But my needs have nothing to do with that."

Again, he was unable to say anything.

"You don't understand. It's always that way with normals." She touched his arm. "Do you know what the leading cause of death is among normal people? Most diseases are curable now, so old age and accidents are the ways ordinary people mostly die. But among exotics, the chief cause of death is murder."

"Murder?"

She nodded. "Yes. Mostly by non-exotics. We are slain by jealous lovers, by cunt- or dickmasters who sell us, by the envious who wish they could be like us. Three of five exotics who die are killed—sometimes we kill each other."

"I—I—didn't realize—"

"Of course not. Because of what we are, of what we do, we become targets of those around us."

"But—couldn't you . . . tone it down? There must be drugs or therapy which could—"

"—stop our sexual drives? Yes, there are. But would you choose such an option? And even if you did, you might find it was no real cure. We are still desired. As you desire me now, despite all I have said."

Khadaji felt guilty. He did want her, he had an erection, he was ready.

She continued. "I could take combinations of hormones and pheromone suppressants and other chems, and become a kind of normal. I could dye my skin and hair, wear colored lenses and look and act normal. If I wanted to.

"If I wanted to. But I don't want to. I like being attractive, I enjoy bedding lovers, men and women, it's what I am. If you love me, you will have to learn to accept it."

A thought loomed, then, something Khadaji didn't want to consider. But once alive, the thing would not die. "Did you have me become your lover because I could protect you from people like the freight handler? Or the *cunt*master?"

"You saved my life," she said. "I wanted to be grateful in the best way I knew how. And, later, I wanted to continue, because you are a good lover. But—certainly I considered your physical abilities an asset."

He felt dull. Blind, deaf and stupid, that's you, isn't it, Khadaji?

"I am sorry if I have hurt you, Emile. I do think you are a lovely boy."

"I'm a man, not a boy!"

"Then act as a man. Consider what we exchange and decide if it is enough. I told you before I have learned to look out for myself. You must understand this." She allowed her hand to drop and touch the front of his pants lightly.

He felt his already stiff penis jump as she moved her hand away. He wanted to turn and walk away from her, he felt betrayed, he wanted to tell her he would not play her game. But he did not.

When Juete left work, Khadaji followed her.

Their lovemaking had never been so intense, so good.

Afterward, when she was asleep, he cried softly. What was he going to do? He had thought she was to be his, eternally, that she loved him as he did her. Could he learn to live with her lovers, with the things which drove her so differently than he was driven? He thought that he could. It would still be better than any relationship he had ever had, but it would not be what he first thought it would be.

He had been naive, he understood now. Something Pen had said came back to him. He needed other teachers. Well. He had learned something. About himself. From her.

He looked at Juete, her perfect whiteness nestled under the black silk of her sheets. She was beautiful and he did love her. But it was not the same as before.

Not the same.

TWELVE ─────────

THE COMFORTABLE RHYTHM of work, exercise and Juete remained the same, on the surface. The work was becoming easier, almost dull. Now and again, there would be something he had to look up, but mostly, he was able to do in two minutes what would have taken ten a few months earlier. The sumito exercises felt solid, he practiced them daily and his control increased slowly and steadily. And Juete was as good as ever. She was discreet; Khadaji never knew for certain when she had lovers. He was sure she did meet other men and maybe women, when they were not together. She spent most of her off-time with him, but not all of it. He wanted to ask, but he never did. He could stand it, if he didn't have to know. When he thought about it, he was honest enough to know his imagination had to be painting a much worse picture than the truth. But he could stand it.

The days and weeks slipped by in a monochromatic routine which became his security. The highs were few, but then, so were the lows. Work. Exercise. Juete. There was no major factor against which he could complain, nothing was really wrong, there were no sharp points of discontent jabbing at him. He lived day to day, in a kind of fuzzy disquiet.

Eventually, it was a customer who brought things to a focal point for Khadaji, an old woman lost in the depths of expensive wine. She spoke to Khadaji because he was there; he thought she would have said as much to the wall, had he not been.

"—nine'y-seven, boy, that's how old. I might have—wha?—another twenny-five years lef'? Tha' be all righ', I had the body I did when I was for—for*ty!* But like this? Why should I bother? I could'uh been so much more, y'know? I had chances, I could—could—have gone to Earth, been the mis'ress of a rich bi'ch. I could'uh been powerful, rich, *some*body! Bu' I pissed it away, I din wanna take the chance. I thought I'd have time, plen'y of time, I was young, I was forty! An' now I'm old and it's all gone pas' an' it's too late."

She looked up from the glass of clear wine and stared at Khadaji, who stood silently behind the bar. The pub was nearly empty and he had no chem to mix.

"But you don' unnerstan'. You're a kid, you think you've got all the time there is, don'cha? Blow off a year here, piss away a year there, it don' matter, you got plen'y to spare."

She lifted the wine glass, drained it, and set it carefully back onto the bright surface of the bar, as if it were still full and she was afraid of spilling it. "But you're wrong. Wrong."

Khadaji nodded, but it was more for himself than the old woman. There was no flash of sudden knowledge, no cosmic rush of feeling, but there was a moment of . . . focus. Why was he here? Working in a backworld pub, listening to a drunk, nailed into a routine which was comfortable and pleasant, but going nowhere? He tried to think about the feeling he'd had during the battle on Maro, when he'd deserted the military, but that certainty, that sense of purpose, was only a faint memory. When had it faded? Why? He did remember the horror he'd felt at all the killing. A Confederation which could condone such had to be evil. It had to be opposed.

Well. You're certainly in a position to do a lot about it here, aren't you?

"One more," the old lady said.

Khadaji mechanically punched in the order and waited while the dispenser filled the glass with the fermented products of three kinds of grapes. Funny, how deep his knowledge of such things ran. The *cuvee* of this particular liquid was a blend of Pinot Noir, Pinot Meunier and Chardonnay, a single-fermentation process. Given time and another round of fermentation and *tirage,* still wines could become champagnes. He knew this, but he did not know many other things, important things.

"Hurry up, honey, I only got maybe twenny-five years lef', remember?"

He set the glass in front of the woman and added the cost to her credit tab. She clutched the wine with both hands.

Khadaji shook his head. Tending pub wasn't going to teach him how to resist the Confed. He had to educate himself, he had to learn how the beast was built, how to find its Achilles' heel—or if it even had such a weak point. He stared at the old lady and understood what it was she had said. There was so much he needed to know and so little time in which to learn it. He had to start now.

Yes. Now.

Most of the patrons had gone home, including the old woman who liked still wine, and only the hardiest of the vampire crowd remained, talking quietly among themselves. Juete was also gone—and not alone, Khadaji had seen.

When he told Kamus, the old man was philosophical.

"I figured," he said. "You were beginning to get the look. Most tenders are afflicted with itchy feet, I never can keep the good ones very long. I was hoping you'd settle in with Juete and stick for a while longer, but if you're set, I won't kick. I'll give you a good vouch. You'll stay long enough to let me break in a new tender?"

Khadaji nodded. "Sure."

"If it's none of my business, say so, but—where you going?"

"I don't really know, Kamus. I've got some things I need to work out, some studying to do. I thought I might try Bocca, in the Faust System."

"Yeah, well, that's the place to go if you want education. If it's taught anywhere, they teach it on Bocca."

"So I've heard."

The old man looked thoughtful for a moment. "What about Juete? You seem tied to her pretty tight. You plan to try and get her to go with you?"

Khadaji thought about that for a long time before he answered.

He had planned to tell her before they made love, but he didn't want to spoil what might be the last time. Afterward, when they lay quietly in her soft bed, it was easier.

"Leave? Why?"

He had not told anyone before, save Pen, but he tried to explain it to her. He started with his life in the military, told her about his feelings before and during and after the slaughter on Maro. About the feeling of . . . wrongness that he had seen, and the knowledge that he must do something about it.

"You are only one man," she said. Her voice was soft.

"A single man cannot hope to change the ways of an entire galaxy."

"You're probably right," he said. "I don't think one man can change it all. But maybe I can affect it some, in some small way."

"You would be a ripple in an ocean, at best."

He sighed. "Maybe. Better a ripple than nothing."

"Bocca is a tropical world," she said. "Hot, rainy, a burning sun. My skin would not survive without constant screening. You would ask me to accept that?"

For a long moment, he said nothing. "Would you go, if I asked?"

She was quiet for a time, as well. Then, "We have been good together. I can see your love for me, and I feel such for you, in my own way. But you're asking me to leave my home, the world of my birth, a place where I am hardly accepted, to go to a place where I would be more of a freak."

He took a deep breath. "No, I'm not asking you to do that."

She sat up suddenly. The servomotors in the bed whined as they tried to adjust to her quick movement. "You *aren't* asking me to go with you?" Her voice was laced with puzzlement—and anger.

"I wanted to know if you would—*if* I were to ask. You didn't seem particularly enthused about the idea, so I won't ask."

Juete slid away from him and out of the bed. She turned and stared down at him, her hands clenched into fists. She was no less beautiful for her anger. Khadaji felt a hard lump gather in his chest, and a dryness wrapped his throat. "You don't *want* me to go!"

He sat up on the bed and clasped his arms around his bare knees. "I love you. I want to stay with you. But I also have something I must do. I have a . . . vision. I might well fail in trying to attain that vision. Probably I will. I can't ask you to share the kind of life I might have."

"You can't ask?—" Her voice became cold, as it did when he'd seen her really angry. "I would not have gone. If you had begged, I would not have gone!"

In that moment, looking at her wonderful nakedness, he thought he understood something more about her. She needed him to ask her to go, so *she* could be the one to refuse. He had known she wouldn't leave Darkworld and so had thought to spare his own ego by playing 'what if' games with her. In doing so, he had cheated her of refusing. It was an important point, one he should remember. He was tempted to say something, to tell her she would do just fine without him, that she could find another like him with little effort. But he didn't say it; it was a thing they both knew. And there were already others.

He slid off the bed and began to gather his clothes.

They did not speak as he dressed. He realized now that he had not really known Juete as he had thought.

Already, he was learning.

There was no one to see him off at the sling. As Khadaji stood there, waiting to board the boxcar, he wondered if Pen had known this moment would come. He wondered about Pen, about how he was doing, where he was. There might be a way to trace him, through the Siblings of the Shroud. One day, he would have to do that. But not now. Now, he had places to go and things to learn, it was time to start thinking of what he was going to do, and how it might be achieved, once he decided. Leaving Juete was painful, but he would survive. It was as Pen had said: the Disk was still in spin and who could say where it would take him?

His inner voice spoke to him then, nasty in its interrogative. *O how philosophical we are! Would you have been so quick to leave if you'd thought Juete 'faithful' to you? Was it your vision which truly made you go? Or lanced pride?*

Khadaji shook his head, but the voice had already done its mischief and was gone. He didn't want to think about the question it had raised. Damn!

As he entered the boxcar, he half-hoped to see Juete running up to the entrance, to ask him to stay—or to go with him. It didn't happen. Self-control, Pen had taught him, was primary. You had to be able to control your own actions before you could hope to influence the actions of others.

He had, Khadaji knew, kilometers and years to go.

Ah, damn!

THIRTEEN ————————

KHADAJI STROKED A control bar and the form-chair in which
he sat extruded itself into a bed, complete with privacy
sonics and polarizers. He was tired, more so than he should
be after only six hours on the system hopper. He wanted to
be alone.

The voyage from Rim to Bocca would take six days.
That time would be on both ends of the trip, moving at
subluminal speeds before and after the Bender did its magic.
Bender was what it was called by almost everybody, but
the true name of the drive which gave men the galaxy was
the Scates-Waller Augmented Reality Analog Instigation
Construct. What it did was simple enough to say—the Bender
put a ship into that state of being in which the vessel was
all places at once. Once there (or here or everywhere), the
Bender wrapped metaphysical fingers around a particular
point of allness and pulled it to the ship. The physics and
mathematics of it were enough to drive an average genius

insane—Scates and Waller had both been as far above the
average genius as the average genius was above a moron.

*So what, Khadaji? Why do you care? Aren't you just
trying to avoid what you really should be thinking about?
Hmmm?*

Yes, dammit! Leave me be!

Maybe the bed was a bad idea, he thought. Maybe he
should go to the lounge and strike up a conversation with
another passenger.

No. He didn't want to do that.

He looked at the menu on the bed's control holoproj and
saw that the device had a built-in sleep generator. Good.
He would set the thing for six hours and escape his thoughts
that way.

It was only as he was drifting off that Khadaji wondered
what he might dream about. . . .

—was deep enough so the warmer colors had begun to fade,
save under the artificial day of the lamps he wore. There
were left the blues and violets, rippling gently in the cold
silk of the Nemui Sea. Emile wondered about that name.
The oceans of San Yubi were all connected and at times,
this named portion of the water world seemed anything but
a Sleepy Sea.

"Emile, let's have a position report."

The voice from his comset startled the boy. He glanced
at the chronographic read built into the rim of his mask.
The numbers winked at him grayly. Sharkshit, he was over-
due again. He cleared his throat. "I'm at hex seven, Dad.
One-nine-two meters."

The suit's heater kicked on, fighting the chill of the water.
Emile still felt cold; probably because his father would be
pissed at him for missing report-in time as much as from
the water.

"Recorded," his father said. "Do let me know when you

reach the inversion, if you are still awake."

"Yes, sir." He felt guilty enough without the sarcasm. The old man could really be nasty when he wanted to be. Good thing his mother wasn't oncom. She was already pissed at them both. She didn't want Emile doing visuals any deeper than a hundred meters anyway; if she knew he was past-tensing his reports, she'd raise bottom muck to get the old man to cancel it.

Emile blew a larger than normal exhaust. The bitter tasting gas mix chorused away from him in a burst of hemispherical bubbles heading for the surface. His mother was relatively dense, considering she was a medic and a lib. Half of Emile's friends were doing deep visuals, easy, and he'd been dolphed by them until his old man had finally let him go below a hundred. Sharkshit, he was twelve, not a towhead!

Emile looked down, but it was too dark to see the inversion layer yet. He checked his descent rate, adjusted the suit's trim a hair to speed it up.

'Course, there was good and bad in being able to do deep. He *wanted* to, but he also didn't want the old man to think he'd changed his mind about herding. No way. There were five other worlds in the Shin System and he'd never even been off planet. He didn't want to spend his life sucking mix and herding tuna. Directing sharks and harvesting was fun, but it got old fast. He didn't know how the old man kept it up after all the years. It was flatshoal boring and Emile wasn't going to spend his life doing it— not studying and cataloging ick and bug poisons like his mother, either. He pitied his little sister. Evin already had it laid out for her, she'd be a fishfarmer, contracted to a fishfarmer, and when she got old enough to get pregnant, she'd raise more fishfarmers! Sharkshit, it was enough to make him want to spit. He was getting out and off, soon as he was able.

Meanwhile, he'd better not miss another report. Emile kept a steady watch on his chronometric read as he sank toward the inversion layer.

—slid the hatch of the bottle shut and tapped the sealer control. He grinned like a dolph through the densecris dome at the approaching storm. It looked like a good one, and Weather had reported the pod was thick and full of juice.

"Yo, Emile, you tucked and ready?"

Emile laughed. That was Little Hamay in his bottle. He was half a klick south and behind Emile's bottle, so he couldn't see the other boy, but Emile said, "Yeah, I'm ready."

Already the bottle began to bob in the small waves being pushed ahead of the storm. It looked like it was gonna be a good fucking ride. Lightning flared two klicks away.

A third voice filled the short circ of the com. "Are you sure we won't get into deepmuck over this?" That was Jeda, in her own bottle, just to Emile's left.

"No way," Emile said. "I told 'em we'd be discom while we ran the desal tests, so we got three hours, at least. Nobody will bother us and we can dive and be back on station in plenty of time to finish."

"You hope."

"Trust me, Jeda. I wouldn't lie to you." Talking to Jeda made him feel tingly, as if something was fluttering in his belly. Last year, she'd been just another girl. But now, there was something different about her. He hadn't figured out just what had changed, but something sure had. He kept wanting to be around her, to talk, to be . . . alone with her. Only most of the time, he couldn't think of a sharkshitting thing to say. So he'd invited her to storm-bounce with him and Little Hamay. "What'd you have to ask her along for?" Little Hamay had said. All Emile could do was shrug. Why not?

The rain came across the water in blowing patterns, spat-

tering the waves and whitecapping them. Emile's bottle—
a two-meter-long sub shaped like a kayak with a densecris
bubble in the middle—began to pitch a little more. Storm-
bouncing was a kick, but definitely a negative as far as the
adults were concerned. If they knew about this, Emile would
be stuck in his cube and disconnected from anything except
edcom for two weeks. But they wouldn't find out.

Little Hamay came oncom. "Hey, Emile, you heard the
story about the Deep Ranger?"

Deep Ranger was the hero of the entcom series cast. Guy
was able to change into a gill suit and kick ass like nobody
when the mals started trouble. He wore a disguise, so nobody would know his secret identity. "Tell me," Emile said.

"Okay. It's a Fuggin Roy joke. Fuggin Roy is tapped
into edcom, see, and it's primary sex ed. The teacher says,
'Okay, I need some input examples of sex stuff. So Fuggin
Roy's input circ lights, but the teacher don't want to call
on him, 'cause he's such a jerk-off. So she calls on Mary.
And Mary says, 'Mitosis, that's cell division.' And the
teacher says, 'Good, Mary. Who else?' And Fuggin Roy's
circ blares again, but she calls on Bill, and he lays out
something about menstrual periods. 'Good,' she says. 'One
more.' This time, nobody's circ lights except Fuggin Roy,
so she has to call on him. So Fuggin Roy says, 'Well, the
Deep Ranger is out diving, see, and all of a sudden, eight
thousand mals come out of the coral and start shooting at
him with harpguns. So the Deep Ranger pulls his own harp-
gun and starts filling the water with long darts, zap, zap,
zap! And pretty soon, the Deep Ranger has killed all the
mals, speared 'em deader than chum.' The teacher waits a
few seconds and Fuggin Roy don't say nothing else, so she
says, 'Well, that's a very nice story, Roy, but—what's it
got to do with sex?' And Fuggin Roy says, 'Well, it'll teach
them mals not to fuck with the Deep Ranger!'"

Emile wanted to laugh, but he held it, waiting to hear

how Jeda was going to react. After a second, she came oncom. "That's stupid, Hamay, really stupid."

Emile didn't say anything—his bottle was sliding down the trough of a big wave and he was trying to hold the nose into the wind. It wasn't that stupid a joke, really. Actually, it was kind of funny, but he didn't laugh. Suddenly, what Jeda thought of him seemed more important than what Little Hamay, his friend for years, thought. And his gut churned in a funny way that was only partially due to the sudden roll of the bottle as the storm clawed at it.

"—your duty to the Confederation *requires* your participation in galactic service. You should all know the alternatives by now, but I will list them again." The Confed rep stood in the center of the assembly hall in front of an active holoproj unit. The two hundred seats were filled with young men and women, all watching the rep. Emile Khadaji watched maybe a little more carefully than most.

"First, there's the military. Confed standard is six years. Then there's medical, you've got eight years' tour there. Those of you with weak stomachs can try for Civilian Corps, but the input is limited and we are talking about ten years minimum. That's it, people. You *will* have to do your duty, one way or another. It's up to you. Personally, I would hope you'd do military. The pay is better, the chances for advancement better, and the tour is shorter. Who knows? You might even get posted to your homeworld."

Several people laughed at this. The military contingent on San Yubi consisted of a hundred troopers; chances of anybody here making it into that post were slim and snowball. Besides, Emile didn't want to be stuck on his homeworld. He wanted to see the galaxy, he wanted to see action.

Jeda leaned toward Emile from her seat next to him. "Medical is the best deal."

Emile smiled, but said nothing. They talked about joining

Medical together and asking for link-posting. But Jeda wasn't as . . . exciting as she'd once been. She was, Emile reflected, kind of . . . dull. He'd had other girls, even a few guys, to play nik-nik games with since that first time with her, and, well, she wasn't so hot. He was going for Military, for a new start. One thing he had learned: there *were* a lot of fish in the sea. He meant to sample a few. . . .

"—won't hurt, but you may notice a transient itching sensation," the Medic said.

The goddamned fishfucker! 'Transient itching sensation,' was it? Khadaji felt as if someone had pumped him full of rock venom. It was all he could do to keep from clawing gouges in his skin. Each of the fucking bacteria must have teeth and talons!

But the augmentation process was working. He tried the test he'd heard about, the stack of coins on the back of his hand. When he dropped his hand from under the metal circles, it seemed as if he had all the time in the galaxy to pluck them from the air. Oh, he was fast! Of course, it didn't make much difference in the barracks, since everybody else was auged the same way, but against a civilian? He couldn't wait to get to a pub to start a fight.

The military minds weren't completely stupid, though. Until the newness wore off, speed-augmented troopers were kept away from civilians. Too fucking bad. . . .

"A guard? I don't want to be a fucking *guard,* Sub!"

"Seal it, Khadaji. None of us want to be guards. But the Confed in its wisdom has seen fit to bend us to Kontrau'lega for a time. You *will* make the best of it."

Khadaji turned to his bunkmate, Theris. "Shit. After Nazo I thought they'd send us where we could see more action. We're battle-tested, experienced!"

The small dark woman looked up at him. "So are half

the ground forces in the system, Emilio, old dork. Way I hear it, Kontrau'lega is a reward for a job well done."

"Shit."

—airgun barked and Khadaji saw Theris's left eye disappear. She fell, and he swept his carbine in a semicircle at hip level, firing on full auto. A dozen of the breakers were stopped by the lead wall, and the closer prisoners were blown apart by the explosive rounds.

"Theris!" Khadaji dropped, oblivious to the roar around him. He stabbed his thumb and forefinger at her carotids, but there was no pulse. The steel pellet must have gone right into her brain, she was dead before she touched the neatly clipped lawn.

When he stood, his rage was in full charge. The fuckers were going to pay for Theris, every goddamned one of them—

"—don't *want* me to go!
"—*want* me—!
"—don't—!"

Khadaji came up from the sonically-induced sleep, fighting the dream. The pure white skin and flowing white hair of Juete filled his mind, along with her rage at being deserted. *You should have let me refuse,* she seemed to say. *You owed me that much.*

Khadaji lay quietly in the bed for a moment, allowing his heart to slow to normal. Sleeping was not the answer, not if it brought dreams. His past was not going to help him now. He had to start anew, to begin on the path he'd seen tantilizing him on Maro. He had to *do* something.

It was going to be a long trip to Bocca, he realized. Far longer than he'd expected.

FOURTEEN ————————

A TROPICAL THUNDERSTORM was in full rage as the shuttle landed at the port of Nagas on Bocca. The attendants on the boxcar were moving among the passengers with hoops of reverse-os thinfilm. Khadaji stood as the young woman approached and raised the hoop over his head.

"Hold your breath for a second," she said.

Khadaji took a deep breath and the woman brought the hoop down slowly around his body until it touched the deck. Khadaji stepped over the edge of the hoop and the woman raised it and moved to the next passenger.

The microthin plastic felt like cobwebs on his skin, and Khadaji quickly cleared his mouth and nostrils so it wouldn't be sucked in when he breathed. The thinfilm sheet had already conformed to his body to form a water-repellent layer. It had a half-life of ten minutes before it would begin to die, but it would keep him dry long enough to reach the terminal. In twenty minutes, the material would be completely gone, evaporated harmlessly into the air.

The rain pounded at him as Khadaji walked quickly to the terminal. It was hot, the rain was nearly as warm as the air, and hard flashes of lightning were followed quickly by sheet-metal rolls of thunder. It was hard to see much, and Khadaji followed the passenger in front of him. A gust of wind shook him as he reached the terminal.

Inside, the customs officer checked him through.

"Purpose of your visit?"

"Student," Khadaji said.

The man looked bored. Bocca's single major industry was knowledge, in one form or another. "Subject?"

Khadaji didn't speak for a few seconds. He hadn't really decided, yet. He had some vague ideas, but nothing for certain. What was he going to study?

The customs man began to look irritated.

"Politics," Khadaji said suddenly.

The man nodded, bored again. He returned Khadaji's tag and waved him through.

It seemed as if the whole damned planet was a university. There were thousands of colleges, covering tens of thousands of subjects. Khadaji stared at the catalogue scrolling across the holoproj image. Politics? What kind? There were dozens of choices: Human or Mutant? Current or Past? System? Planet? State? Theoretical? And, assuming he could choose a particular branch, there were several ways to go about learning the material, too. Viral Inject. Hypnotic Induct. Real Time.

Viral Inject was the fastest. A few minutes and you could absorb an entire course, coded into educational virus which would become a part of your own nervous system. Hypnosis took longer, several sessions of an hour or so, but the information was the same and locked in fairly well. Real Time was the chanciest, there were no guarantees because the

work had to be done by the student. Well, Viral seemed
like the way to go—until Khadaji saw the prices. Buddha
and Jackson! He'd saved most of the money he'd earned in
the pub, but a single course would take all of that and more.
Hypnotic courses were cheaper, but still more than he had
to spend. He could afford Real Time, that was all, and not
too much of that. Holy Allah, education was expensive.
He'd never thought much about it before: on his homeworld,
he'd been schooled for free as a child, and part of his father's
benefit package had given Khadaji secondary training in
BasicLib—a total of fifteen years, all for free. He wished
he had some of that free time coming to him now.

The instructor was a pinched-faced woman of eighty, with
frizzy short hair dyed brilliant green in a fashion which was
fifteen years out-of-date. She faced four hundred students
in the auditorium and gave her first and final lecture on
politics.

"There are three files," she said, waving at the air. A
giant holoproj lit to her right, with the names. Khadaji
pointed his comp at the image and pushed the inducer. At
the same time, he heard several hundred other inducers click
into operation. It sounded like a swarm of angry insects.
The files were dutifully copied by his portable unit.

"Read them carefully," the professor said. "Introduction
to Basic Terran Politics will hold its final examination in
six weeks. The schedules will be filed under class times in
the library's mainframe matrix." With that, the professor
waved her hand again, wiping the holoproj image away.
She turned, and walked from the auditorium.

Next to him, a jet-skinned boy of sixteen or so muttered,
"Shit. I'm gonna line my parents for Viral stads. I hate this
Real Time suck."

Khadaji stared at the names projected above his comp.

•   •   •

THE PRINCE - NICCOLO MACHIAVELLI - 6934561-POL-1
A BOOK OF FIVE RINGS - MIYAMOTO MUSASHI - 7105436-POL-1
THE ART OF COMPROMISE - CARLOS PERITO - 3451509-POL-1

Khadaji looked at the boy and raised an eyebrow.

"That's it," the boy said. "She gives us the reading, we do it, they test us at the end. They're trying to weed us out, there's too many of us, so seal it, you can bet your orbs the test will be a humming peter!"

Khadaji only nodded. It didn't matter to him if he passed the test or not. He wasn't here to get a degree; he was here to learn. Three files. It didn't seem as if he would be able to learn much about politics from them.

He was wrong. Machiavelli had been something called an Italian, and he wrote his theories in pre-Galactic times, but his insight was fascinating. Much of the text first seemed incomprehensible, due to archaic references to Terran sub-states like France and Rome and Tuscany, but Khadaji was able to decipher those using a basic history file in the library. The more he read, the more he understood.

Musashi's book was concerned with sword fighting, of all things. But a deeper look showed strategy beyond that of waving a sharp metal blade. Khadaji couldn't help remembering Pen's lessons with the curved knife, back on the Darkworld.

Perito was an early post-Galactic, writing on Alpha Point in the Centauri System. His psychological insights delved deeper than the others, and he talked much of ethics.

Amazing, that such men could know so much. It made Khadaji realize how little he knew.

Military Science was structured differently. There were regular class sessions with a live instructor, and Khadaji felt almost at home in the classes. He had, after all, been a soldier. He was done with that, but since the Military was the enforcement arm of the Confed, it seemed like a good idea to learn as much as he could about it.

"—is your basic antipersonnel, fully automatic, blowback-operated shoulder weapon," the instructor droned in a bored voice. "It holds five hunnert rounds of point one-seven-seven explosive ammunition with a rate of fire of eight rounds per second. This here shoulder weapon weighs three point six three kilograms empty and five point one kilograms fully loaded. People, this is your weapon, not your gun." He waved the Parker in the air. "This is for work." He dropped one hand to touch himself on the crotch. "This is for fun. Don't mistake one for the other. Those of you not male or electively equipped as such might remember that easier."

Khadaji found a small bar in the town serving the university branch and managed to get hired as a backup tender. The pay wasn't that good, but the job included a communal sleeping room and at least one meal a day. The money he had saved from Kamus wouldn't last forever, and, it seemed, there was a lot he didn't know. The vastness of human knowledge seemed like some monstrous void looming in front of him. He was ignorant, he realized, and ill-equipped to challenge a galactic Confederation in any area.

From politics, Khadaji naturally slid into the study of history; then came psychology, sociology, biology and sociobiology. He delivered drinks and powders in the pub by day and attended classes and worked the library comp in the evenings. He took classes in physics and chemistry, in electronics and atomic theory; he learned about warps and drives; he immersed himself in astronomy and astrophysics. The more he learned, the more he wanted to learn. Knowledge became a joy for him, an end in itself. Time went by in a

kind of intellectual blur, filled with something new each
day. A line of study would often take a turn, dragging
Khadaji into a new discipline which would blossom for him,
making him grin as he tapped the controls of the comp and
chased the information like a predator chasing prey. Astronomy, astrophysics, medicine, religion; they all called to
him. . . .

Confederation History: now there was a subject. Khadaji
had paid little attention to such things before; after all, the
Confed was so vast and ever-present, it was like worrying
about breathing. On screen, the dates and facts were dry
and lifeless: the first extee colony off Earth, 2000 A.D.;
the first ship to reach another stellar system, the ill-fated
Heaven Star, constructed in space and launched in 2072; in
2193, the Bender Drive was perfected, giving FTL travel.
Then came the leap: from 2195 to 2255, there was the
Expansion, a period of intense colonization; from 2255 to
2295, the Consolidation held sway, in which the galactic
association became more rigid, less a loose association and
more a bureaucracy. And, although the Confed frowned
deeply upon it, the period since 2295 was becoming known
as the Declination. The fifty-six planets and eighty-seven
wheel worlds were growing ever more restless. In the spiral
Sb which is the Milky Way, such a Confederation was less
than a scratch upon the hundred billion stars which formed
the galaxy; still, the Confed was spread over a thousand
light years, and even at its fastest, the Bender took time.
And what the official histories usually left out was the sense
of oppression ordinary people felt from the vastness of the
indifferent Confed. The beast had long since stopped serving
to become the master. The Confed did what governments
were famed for: it made more government. To oppose it
was treason, and worth death. Even a monster has fear.

•   •   •

"—etiology of the pathogen was at first unknown, but experiments revealed that the viral matrix was consistent with that of an opportunistic symbiote of the class—"

"—type of geological formation is only found in areas of volcanic activity—"

"—of which tantric is the most popular form—"

"—subatomic realm we must deal in theory—"

"—me a Bloody Mary, would you Emile? My fucking head feels like it's going to fucking explode!"

Khadaji grinned and began to construct the drink. It was fairly busy, but not too bad. The pub was quiet as it almost always was—the college crowd would sometimes get loud, but usually only during the period around exams. Maurice, the owner, didn't even have a full-time bouncer. He hired an off-duty pol when he thought things might get rowdy.

Three people came in while Khadaji was making the Bloody Mary, all dressed in Confed military uniforms. He felt the short rush of coldness in his gut he usually did when he saw legit Military—after all, he was a deserter. It might be half a galaxy away from Maro, but Bocca was a kind of crossroads. He was aware of the small chance of encountering somebody he knew whenever he saw a uniformed trooper.

The coldness faded. The three—two women and a man—were young, maybe twenty or so, and so wouldn't know him. It had been six years since Maro.

That stopped him. Six years? That meant he had been studying here on Bocca for—what?—four years? At least that. He blinked at the realization. Where had the time gone? He hadn't begun to make a dent in what there was to be learned. He was still a young man, only thirty-two, but— six years?

Khadaji felt a break in the normal rhythms of the pub. Something was going on, something unusual. He glanced around. A soldier was standing, one of the women, glaring down at a single man at a table near where the other two soldiers still sat. The woman was angry.

Khadaji tried to tune out the background noises of the pub so he could hear her.

"—much care for the way you stared at us when we came in, chickie. What the hell do you think you're looking at?"

The man, a slightly built redhead, shook his head. Khadaji didn't recognize him, he wasn't one of the regulars.

"Sorry," he said. He had some kind of accent Khadaji couldn't place right away. Baszelian, maybe? "No offense meant."

"Yeah, well I don't think much of your manners, chickie. And I think you were eyeing my partner too much." The soldier waved at the second woman sitting behind her.

Khadaji began to work his way to the end of the bar. He could see trouble. The woman had already been into chem somewhere. From her sleeve insignia, he could see she was a combat vet; Khadaji was willing to bet the other two were, as well. All three wore air pistols clamped into plastic spring holsters.

"Like I said, I'm sorry, I didn't mean to offer insult," the redhead said. He had his hands palm up on the table. Khadaji noticed his right index finger was curled almost to his palm.

"I think I just might kick your ass," the trooper said. "Right here and right now."

The redhead said nothing, but shook his head.

"No? You don't think I can?" The woman was psyching herself up to jump the man. Khadaji rounded the corner of the bar and started toward her. The confrontation had developed an audience by this time.

The trooper bent and grabbed the redhead's tunic and dragged him up from the chair. As she did, he brought his hands around in short arcs and smacked her on both ears with his palms. She screamed and released him. Khadaji grinned. That was a nice move—

Suddenly, the other two troopers kicked away from the table and reached for their air pistols. The woman with the sore ears dug for her own weapon. Buddha, they were going to start shooting! Khadaji sprinted, hoping to reach them before they killed the redhead.

The redhead waved his hand back and forth, pointing his finger at the troopers. There were three coughs, a sound like a giant might make spitting. The three troopers fell, knocking over a table and two chairs, their air pistols in their hands but not yet clear of the clamps on their hips. What—?

The man with red hair came out of a shooter's crouch, but Khadaji didn't see a weapon. The man's hands were empty, no way could he have drawn a weapon, fired three times, and put it away without Khadaji seeing it.

Red saw Khadaji approaching and shifted his stance slightly toward him.

"Easy," Khadaji said, holding his hands in sight, fingers spread wide. "You're clear, they went for firepower first."

Red seemed to relax slightly. He nodded, but didn't smile.

When Khadaji was two meters away, he stopped. "The sector pol works for us as a bouncer sometimes. We'll call it self-protection—he'll go along with that."

Red nodded. "I'd just as soon not get involved with the local cools. Or the Confed Military pols. Maybe I'll bend before they show up."

Khadaji shrugged. "I'm not going to try and stop you." He grinned.

The smaller man smiled back at him, and turned toward the exit.

"One thing before you go," Khadaji said. "What did you hit them with?"

Red turned his right hand, so the back of it faced Khadaji. There was an angular parallelogram riding there, a diamond shape maybe six or seven centimeters on a side, with what looked like a slunglas tube extending from the end in a line with the index finger. The tube was a centimeter longer than Red's finger, and was obviously a barrel for projectiles. The body of the unit was covered in flesh-colored orthoplastic, save for what must be a magazine and its snap-out button.

"Spetsdöd," Red said. "I'm running shocktox darts. They'll be out for fifteen minutes."

They heard the whine of a military ground-effect car, and Red dropped his hand and looked at Khadaji. "Back way out?"

"Through there."

When the military pols blew in, Red was a minute gone. Khadaji stalled in telling of the shoot long enough for him to get further away. After the pols and medics were through, Khadaji thought about what he had seen. There was something important in it, something he couldn't quite grasp.

FIFTEEN ⸻

IT WAS RAINING again. The pounding tropical downpour was punctuated with heavy electrical discharges and the resulting clap of air rushing in to fill the void left by the lightning. Thick-leaved trees danced and swayed under the windy sheets and puddles expanded into miniature seas, drowning gray plastcrete streets and walks.

Khadaji liked the rain. It reminded him of his homeworld. As a boy, he would watch the storms, sometimes with waterspouts, sweep across the ocean as if they were living things. Rain cleaned the air, refreshed the ions, and stirred the fish. It was always more fun to work the schools after a heavy rain, the mock-tuna seemed more frantic, the poda's oxy streamers were fully extended, even the guard sharks roused from their normal lethargy. And it wasn't just within a few meters of the surface, either. The deep fish knew about the rain, somehow, and they showed it.

Khadaji sat under the wide overhang of a pagoda roof,

watching the rain. The wind blew spray at him now and
again, but he was mostly dry. People walked or ran by
wrapped in micro-plastic sheets or carrying umbrel-fields;
life couldn't stop because of the rain. In another few years,
so they said, weather control would be installed on Bocca,
and the storms would be scheduled and milder. So they said.

Khadaji sighed. If he considered his life since his Realization on Maro as a mountain climb, then he was certainly
taking a lot of time to look at the rocks and caves along the
way. First it had been Pen, then Juete, and now it was the
seductive lure of education. There was inside him the drive
to *do* something, even though he did not know what. What
he did know was that he wasn't moving. Sure, he was
learning a lot—had learned a lot from all his experiences—
but running through it all was a feeling of frustration.

Lightning scored the air maybe two hundred meters away,
striking up at the clouds from a bleeder tower designed for
that purpose. The thunder fired like a giant's carbine and
the sound seemed to shake more rain from the dark clouds.
A short mue dressed in phosphor gear ran by, cursing the
weather, as she splashed through the sea-over-plastcrete.

He remembered the fight in the pub vividly. The three
troopers going for weapons and being blown down by a
single man with what amounted to an air-powered dart gun.
Sure, they were chem-lit, but they were also combat vets,
highly trained and deadly. And Red had taken them, quickly
and efficiently, without raising perspiration. The Confed
wasn't invincible: He'd been a trooper, he knew that. There
were too many soldiers for any person or group to resist
openly, that would be suicide.

He thought about the killing he'd seen, about his final
participation in the slaughter on Maro. It still made him
want to vomit, the thought of all those people ceasing to
exist. Many religions had it that there was another life,
another existence following the one known, but Khadaji

held no faith in that idea. Maybe so, maybe not. It would be nice, but until it was proven, a person should make the best of his or her time on the physical plane. And if all those dead on Maro were wrong?. . . . Then they were wasted, like a shipment of bad foodstuffs or contaminated chem. That felt so wrong to him there were no words for it. Any type of violence initiated by one intelligent being against another was wrong. Killing violence was worse than any other kind. How could it be condoned? In his brief moment of cosmic bliss, Khadaji had *seen* the value of intelligent life. Man and his self-created mues were alone in the galaxy as evolved intelligence. Certainly, there were artificials— computers and genetically altered animals—but no aliens had been discovered above the level of an unaltered dog. It was a big galaxy, plenty of room for every human or neo-human, it wasn't necessary to kill any of them!

The rain continued to pound the trees and buildings and ground; Khadaji's shoulders were tense and drawn up. He took a deep breath and relaxed as he exhaled both air and anger. Somebody had to do something. Somebody had to stop the Confed, had to make it release its steel grip, had to end its casual death-dealing.

Khadaji laughed into the rain. Who? Him? By himself? Sure. It wasn't just funny, it was a screamer. But he kept seeing Red—who was he? What kind of man was he?— sweeping the three soldiers away. In the end, even the largest army was made up of single units, men and women like those in the pub. Like he himself had been. While no man could stand against the might of the entire Confed, a single man might be able to move against them in smaller numbers, if he were careful, if he were clever and skilled.

The rain began to slacken. The drops were smaller, the wind less; the clouds were nearly empty.

Yes. The time had come to do something. But—no matter how he twisted his thinking, Khadaji could only see one path to effect the kind of changes he wanted and it was not evolution but its faster brother—revolution. And violence was all too integral to that manner of change. The irony of it was not lost on him. I am for peace—do it my way or I'll kill you. . . .

The rain gave a short-lived surge and tried to recapture its glory as a storm, but the effort failed. The last drops fell and the hot sun was revealed by the retreating clouds. Vapor rose from slate roofs and plastcrete, returning to the air to begin the cycle again.

Khadaji stepped from the pagoda and walked in the warmth of the early afternoon. Could he use the same excuse as the Confed—the end justified the means? Sometimes it did, of course, but could one ethically justify using the same methods as a deplored enemy, in order to get it to stop?

Khadaji waded through a puddle which covered his dotics and rose to his ankles. What other paths were there? His studies had shown him that revolution and evolution were the only ways that societies ever truly changed. Revolution and evolution, built of a mix of education and violence and politics and compromise and self-interest and self-preservation. Certainly, history showed that rigid societies, like ancient dinosaurs, always died. The Confed was the biggest dinosaur ever, and while it was already dying and had been doing so for a long time, it would take many years before it finally fell. Any empire which had to hold its citizens in check with military force was far down the road to destruction. Which brought up another thought: what would replace the dead beast when it began to rot? What parasite would emerge from the corpse to try and breed itself into superiority?

Khadaji shook his head. He didn't know enough, he knew that much, but every moment he allowed to pass without action meant it was that much less likely he would accomplish anything. It was time to do something.

What, and how?—those were puzzles still to be solved.

He grinned to himself. Funny, how much he had changed in the last few years. Who would have ever guessed at what he was now planning and doing, compared to what he thought and did as a callow young soldier? Certainly not one Emile Antoon Khadaji. It had all sprung from one cosmic moment on a battlefield, something no one would have ever foreseen. Based on that one flash of knowledge and the subsequent faith attached, he had altered his life dramatically. He'd become a deserter; he'd educated himself in processes he'd never known about; he now contemplated unthinkable acts. Such things were utterly amazing, even now. That spiritual moment drove him, forcing him to become more than he'd ever dreamed he would be. In a way, he had become a kind of intellectual; it was time now for him to become much more active.

It took him two weeks to find Red. And even then, it was more a matter of luck than Khadaji's skill as an investigator. He had read the texts on detection and investigation, but there were some things which didn't translate well from a text file. "Contact local sources of information" was a lot easier in theory than it was in practice.

Red wasn't particularly thrilled to see him.

They met in a somatic club, amid rows of people sitting in electrostim units, having their muscles exercised. Red was utilizing an old-fashioned set of free weights, and sweating with the effort. Khadaji noticed he wore the spets-död even here.

"Yes?" Red looked wary.

Khadaji explained what he wanted.

"You jest."

"No. I'll pay you to teach me."

"Why?"

"Self-protection."

Red stared at Khadaji's body. Like most of the others in the club, Khadaji wore only a groin strap. His body was better than most; all the hours of sumito practice kept him lean and tight. "You look as if you could take care of yourself, if the need arose."

"Against three armed troopers?"

In answer to that, Red tossed the weight bar he was curling at Khadaji, and brought the spetsdöd up to aim at the bigger man's belly—

Khadaji wasn't there. The weight bar clunked onto the rockfoam floor cover and Red found his outstretched arm clamped at the wrist by a powerful hand; Khadaji was standing next to him, out of the line of fire of the dart shooter. Red grinned widely, and Khadaji released his arm suddenly.

"That's what I thought," Red said. "I saw you move in the pub. You don't need a spetsdöd, friend. You could have taken those three with your hands, no matter if they had air guns, am I right?"

"Probably. But I still want to learn."

Red bent and recovered the weight bar. After curling it several times, he finally spoke. "All right. I'll show you."

As it turned out, Red had a name—Lyle Gatridge—but most people did call him Red. The College of Military Science had an underground weapons range, and they practiced there. The place smelled of lubricant and explosive chem, and it brought back memories of Khadaji's own military training. He could still recall the Sub-Lojt telling the troops to load-and-lock-one-clip-ball-non-explo-and-ready-onna-firing-line.

Killing weapons were generally illegal for civilians in the civilized galaxy, but these weapons which would stun or shock an attacker were allowed, with proper licenses, for self-protection. Tasers, light-cannons and spetsdöds loaded with charged ion-chem were fairly common, Red told Khadaji. He should know, because he earned his money as a bodyguard at times.

"Now you take a taser. It's a fine weapon, it delivers a hard charge which will knock a big man stupid. Problem is, the range is short. A taser's transmitter is only good for maybe fifteen meters, tops. Outside of that, you might as well throw it. There are short-circ vests which will absorb a taser's signal, too.

"Light cannons are fine, they'll blind you, especially at night, just like a photon flare. Problem there is, they're not so good in bright sunshine, and you can wear polarizing contacts which will pretty much kill the effect."

Red handed Khadaji a spetsdöd. "Put it on the back of your hand—this is a right-side model—you peel the backing on the flesh and mold it, like this."

Khadaji wiggled his fingers experimentally. The weapon was very comfortable, light enough so he hardly noticed it was there. The barrel protruded just past the tip of his index finger.

"It's not loaded," Red said, "but you always check that for yourself, don't take anybody's word for it. Right there is where the magazine goes."

Khadaji checked the slot. It was empty.

Red handed him a plastic rectangle about the length of Khadaji's little finger, but only half as thick. "It holds up to fifteen rounds, depending on what kind of dart you load. The power—compressed gas—is built into the magazine. This is stinger ammo—dull-nosed darts without chem. You know you're hit if you get shot by one, but all it does is sting a little; no damage unless it hits an eye or something. Load it with the white end up."

Khadaji obediently snapped the magazine into place.

"That's the eject button next to the magazine. Try it."

Khadaji touched the button and the magazine snapped out and fell onto the floor of the shooting range. Red bent to retrieve it. "You can reload in about three seconds." He returned the magazine and Khadaji reloaded the weapon.

Khadaji dropped his hand next to his thigh and wiggled the fingers again. He had read about how to fire the weapon, there was a chem-sensitive trigger on the end of the barrel which would only react to certain kinds of epidermal tissue, specifically that of a fingernail. There was no safety, unless you wore a fingertip cover.

Red punched in a command on the range computer and a holoproj image lit up three or four meters out. A big man with a knife raised over his head running in place toward them. Khadaji laughed.

"Go ahead, shoot him," Red ordered.

Khadaji nodded and snapped his hand up—and shot himself in the foot.

"Ah, shit! shit, shit, SHIT!"

Red leaned back against the stall support and laughed until tears flowed. "Felt that, did you?"

"Goddammit, that hurt!" Khadaji refrained from hopping around and holding his foot—barely.

"I forgot to mention that the firing mechanism is very sensitive."

"You fishfucker," Khadaji said, glaring at him.

"Ah, ah. You'll remember it better now than if I'd just told you. You see why I always keep my index finger curled in now, don't you?"

"I see."

"How's your foot?"

"I'll live."

"Good. Let's try it again, only take it a little slower, what say?"

It was unlike any weapon Khadaji had ever used in the military. First, the shooting was "instinctive"—it was point-firing, there were no sights, no way to aim. You pointed

your finger at the target and that's where your missile went.
Which was what made it so fast, your target was never any
further away in time than jabbing a finger at it.

A crazed woman waving a hand wand ran on a treadmill
at him. Khadaji pointed his finger at her. A chime rang and
a diode lit on the control panel. A hit.

"Where were you aiming?" Red looked at the board.

"At the woman," Khadaji said dryly.

"*Where* at the woman? Her face? Chest? Left nipple?"

"Her chest."

"You missed, then. You hit her too low, almost at the
navel."

"So? I hit her, didn't I?"

"Not good enough," Red said. "You ever hear the story
of the archers?"

"What's an archer?"

"Bow shooter. Slings an aluminum shaft about a meter
long using the power of a primitive spring—"

"I know what a bow is," Khadaji interrupted.

"Yeah, well there was a contest and the best three archers
in the state were shooting for a prize. The state's ruler had
a big holoproj of a fish hung for a target and the archers
were set back a good distance, fifty or a hundred meters.
So they shot, and one guy won. After the contest, the ruler
called the three archers in one at a time and asked each
archer what he'd been aiming at. The first guy said, 'I was
aiming at the fish.' Second guy said, 'I was aiming at the
middle of the fish.' The third shooter said, 'I was aiming
at the fish's eye.' You want to guess which archer won?"

"Obviously the third archer," Khadaji said.

"Right. Because you only get as accurate as you try for."
He waved his right hand, showing Khadaji his own spetsdöd. "These things have a range of about fifty meters, but
are only effective for maybe half that. Combat range for a
spetsdöd is five to seven meters, that's where you'll do most

of your shooting. You got somebody wearing a vest or
padded 'skins, your only target might be a hand or neck."
Red stopped talking and bent to pick up an empty magazine
from the floor. He held it in the same hand as his spetsdöd,
then casually flipped it into the air downrange.

As Khadaji watched, Red jabbed his finger toward the
tumbling magazine and fired. It jumped away suddenly at
a right angle to its former flight.

"Always aim for the fish's eye, kid. You might not hit
it, but you'll be more likely to hit the fish somewhere."

Getting a license for his own spetsdöd was easy enough.
Khadaji used his own name—in all the billions of people
in the galaxy, there had to be thousands with his name—
and only lied about background. He'd been a citizen and
student on Bocca for four standard years and he had stayed
mostly within local laws. The permit was appended to his
tag and the spetsdöd became a part of his hand. Red had a
left-side model he made Khadaji practice with, sometimes
requiring him to use both at the same time. Khadaji put in
an hour in the range daily, firing off several hundred darts
each session. At first, the improvement in his speed and
accuracy was radical; after a few months, the improvements
came in tiny bits—a half-centimeter closer here, nine hits
instead of eight there. In three months, Khadaji could hit a
tossed magazine six times out of ten.

In six months, he could hit the magazine nine times out
of every ten tosses. He could hit a man-sized target at combat
ranges a hundred times in a row with no misses, and he
could do it standing, sitting or rolling.

In nine months, Khadaji regularly outshot Red, using
either or both hands. He practiced in varied lighting, wearing
heavy and awkward clothing, sometimes blindfolded, shooting at generated sounds from the targets. He still missed
his targets occasionally, but he took each miss as a personal

affront, striving for perfection. The motions of the spetsdöd became almost instinctive, a learned reflex which seemed as natural to him as walking.

"Ready?"

Khadaji nodded, feeling relaxed. He wore spetsdöds on both hands and he held his arms crossed over his chest.

Red stood to Khadaji's left, unmoving. With a sudden jerk, he tossed a handful of empty magazines into the air. Four of the small plastic rectangles glittered in the hard light of the firing range as they tumbled through the air.

Khadaji moved, both arms swinging out, his index fingers stabbing at the small targets, the spetsdöds coughing. He fired four times; there were four hits.

Khadaji grinned. It was easy. He still wasn't sure what he was going to do, but he knew one thing for certain: He was good enough at this, now.

Khadaji was off-duty, so he sat at a table with Red, sipping on his latest experimental drink, champagne. It was really quite good, provided he didn't drink enough to get a headache. Three glasses seemed to be the limit.

"So, what happens now?" Red asked. "You're better than anybody I've ever seen, either with your hands or that." He pointed at the spetsdöd. "Nothing else I can teach you."

"I've got something to do," Khadaji said. "This is only a part of it."

"I thought so."

He didn't ask the obvious question, and Khadaji didn't volunteer. He liked that about Red; the man never pried. Still, Khadaji felt a curiosity about his teacher. "What about you? What did I interrupt?"

Red sipped at his drink. "Not much. I've done a lot of things, mostly dancing around the edges of legality. Bodyguarding, some . . . courier work, freelance odd jobs. Never could find a place interesting enough to settle for more than a few months. You've been interesting, so I've stayed around here, but now that I'm done, I think maybe I'll take off. Lot of galaxy I haven't seen yet."

"No family?"

"Not to speak of. I was married a couple of times, they didn't work out. I have a daughter I've never seen, she'd be her late-teens. Geneva, her name is. I'd like her to have more than the stads I send, but I don't have a lot to offer. Only thing I was ever really good at is what I do."

Khadaji nodded. This was the most he'd learned about Red in all the months he'd known the man. Impulsively, he decided to say something he hadn't planned to say. If anybody could be trusted, it was Red. "Listen, if things go the way I want them to, I might be in a good place in a few years; maybe a place you might want share with your daughter. I'll have a permanent mail code established here, under the name 'Spit Enterprises'." Khadaji smiled "Drop a pulse my way every year or two and let me know where I can find you."

Red grinned. "I was never much for corresponding, kid, but, sure, why the hell not? I can see some kind of fire in you. I dunno what it is, exactly, but something potent. I'll keep in touch."

SIXTEEN ─────────────

KHADAJI SAT IN one of the two thousand booths which made up the main university library, staring at the holoproj image generated by the computer. He knew that if he intended to offer any kind of opposition to the Confederation, it would have to be done from a position of strength. He had a strong body, and certain skill with that body, and now, with a spetsdöd. But more was needed, he had to have some kind of power base.

Power, he'd learned from his study of politics, could come from several sources. It could be military, it could be political, or religious, or it could be money. Often the different kinds were intertwined.

Khadaji touched a control and the heat-sensitive device caused the holoproj to blur as the computer searched for the chosen subject.

Military was out. He'd have to be a Sector Marshal to command any forces strong enough to rise against the Confed and his chances of that were less than those of a snowball in a supernova. Politics would offer no easy access to power, either. It would take too long—assuming he could manage to work his way into an effective political organization. Religion was simply not in the question; he had no bent in that direction at all.

Which left money. It was easier to get rich than it was to get famous, there were a lot of ways to earn standards.

Of course, the trick was to make the money quickly. Within, say, five to ten years. That eliminated most honest work. Starting at the bottom of some corporate lift and rising slowly through the ranks would take some considerable amount of time, even if he had some particular skill in a given field. Which he didn't, really. He was fairly well educated in some areas, but it was mostly academically oriented. And pubtenders didn't die rich.

There were, of course, faster ways to make money honestly. 'Find a need and fill it' was the creed of hundreds of thousands of entrepreneurs throughout history. If one had the proper kind of drive and luck, one could join the ranks of the self-made millionaires.

But the fastest way to make big stads was much simpler. Do it illegally. As always, it seemed that finding illegal needs and filling them paid the best. There were drugs which were frowned upon *here* which could be bought legally *there;* it was then merely a matter of figuring a safe way to transport the chemicals from *here* to *there*. Likewise, there were proscribed weapons, banned holos, illicit sexual devices and a myriad number of things and ideas which were worth a lot to someone able to provide them.

Of course, there were risks involved with such endeavors. Lock-time and brain-diddle weren't pleasant thoughts; neither was being killed by a criminal element which disliked competition. And there were moral issues. Could

Khadaji live with himself were he involved in slavery or life-destroying chemicals?

Of course, laws weren't always just. Some rules outlawed a thing because it was intrinsically bad: child molestation, say. Other rules made harmless activities crimes only because someone wished them to be so. Take cohabitation on a religious holiday. On some worlds, it was legal on one day, illegal the next, and on the third, okay once again. Khadaji could see no moral dilemma there.

The holoproj cleared. The title of the text was: "A Statistical Analysis and Comparison of Activities Violating Major Planetary Laws Involving Crimes Against Property, Indexed by Stellar System."

Khadaji shook his head. The work was, apparently, an ongoing project for graduate-level students, constantly being revised. According to the computer, the file, if printed out, would fill 25,973 pages. As he watched, the number was raised by a hundred. Then another seventy. Even at full *augenblick* speedscan, it would take some time to read it all. He would skim, Khadaji decided, and hit only the highest of the high points. He had no intention of spending the rest of his life trying to read a file which was growing so fast he couldn't keep pace with new additions. . . .

He bought two travel cases that were identical, from a retail outlet which sold thousands of such cases each year. He wore thinskin gloves when handling the cases, so he left no prints or secretions. One case he filled with ordinary items of travel; clothes, toiletries, novel and travel tapes. The second case was filled much the same, but also had several hundred doses of mescabyn hidden in a tape reader. Mescabyn was a mild and harmless hallucinogen, and legal. At least it was legal on Bocca. On the planet's nearest neighbor (and the only other occupied body in the Faust

System), Ago's Moon, the chem was illegal, as were most drugs. If he could get it to the right people, the mescabyn would be worth five hundred times what he had paid for it.

Travel between Bocca and Ago's Moon was easily accomplished and hardly regulated. Naturally, there were smugglers, but inspection of luggage was usually done only on a spot basis. Khadaji bought a fake tag which identified the bearer as Reachardo Hollee and used it to buy a one-way passage to Ago's Moon. He checked the travel case containing the mescabyn through under the new name and had the claim number imprinted on the tag. Immediately, he booked passage on the same commuter ship under his own name, checking the second case. He was quick enough, and the second claim number was sequential to the first. Step one.

Emile Khadaji was more than a little nervous as he sat in the womb-foam of the morning shuttle to Ago's Moon. The attendant offered him a soporific, but he declined. He would have to relax, he thought. If his mental state was apparent, he would be caught for certain.

The ship landed uneventfully and Khadaji proceeded to the luggage claim area. He watched as the bags were ejected through a slot, sometimes fired completely over the conveyer by the robot dins assigned to transport them. Finally, he saw the bag containing the contraband. He was sweating as he reached for the case, expecting at any moment to feel someone clamping hands upon him.

Nothing happened, no one seemed to be watching him, so Khadaji moved to the line waiting to have tags checked against bags. The old woman matching numbers looked bored. The reader she used was not equipped with automatic memory Khadaji knew. That was an important part of his plan. If the device had been so fitted, he would never have tried the caper.

The woman glanced at the readout on the fake tag, saw

the numbers matched, and waved Khadaji through, pointing with her nose. She didn't look at him, but immediately began to check the next man through.

Khadaji released a deep breath. So far, so good. Step two.

The corridor led to customs and there were no exits between the luggage area and the inspection tables. There were, however, small disposal tubes lining the corridor. As inconspicuously as he could, Khadaji approached one of these disposals. He attached a thumbnail-sized sticker of phosphoreme to the fake tag, squeezed it, and dropped it into the wall tube. There was a small *whoosh!* as the tube sucked the plastic tag away, and Khadaji imagined he heard the phosphoreme as it ignited and flashed the ID. Reachardo Hollee no long existed. Step three.

The customs inspectors looked as bored as the woman who checked the claim tags, but Khadaji knew they weren't. This was the most dangerous part. *If* they opened his bag, *if* they found the chem hidden inside the reader, then the caper was aborted. He was, he figured, protected as much as he could be, considering he was guilty of smuggling. He had played the scenario inside his head dozens of times.

"Well, what have we here? Look, Johann, a drug smuggler!"

Khadaji would look astounded. "What? I never saw that before." He would look at the contents of the bag for a moment and the realization would dawn on him. "Hey, wait a minute! That's not my bag!"

"Sure it isn't, chickie. Come over here into my office. Let me see your tag. And move very slowly and carefully when you reach for it, Johann zaps things when he gets nervous."

He would produce his tag, very carefully, trying to look innocent. They would check it.

"Yeah, it's the wrong number, all right. How did you

get it past Marlerra? Giver her a call, Johann. And check to see if there's another bag matching this mumber, too."

After what would seem like a thousand years, the second bag would show up, probably in the company of the old woman. It would be very thoroughly checked, but would be clear of anything illegal. And the number would match. And Khadaji's tag would show he'd only checked one bag through. And they would let him go, though they might be suspicious, and begin looking for Hollee the drug smuggler. . . .

"Your tag," the customs man said, interrupting Khadaji's mental scenario.

"Oh, sorry." He handed the tag over and the man shoved it into a reader.

"Purpose of your visit?"

"Vacation. I'm going to Giant Falls, to do some swimming. Maybe some diving."

"Um. Anything to declare?"

"No sir."

The man pulled Khadaji's tag from the reader and handed it back. He looked at the case Khadaji carried. "That all you're bringing in?"

"Yes sir." Khadaji made as if to put the case onto the inspection table.

The customs man glanced at Khadaji, then at the bag. "Never mind. Have a pleasant time on Ago's Moon." He waved at the next man.

Khadaji forced himself to walk slowly as he moved away from the customs inspector. He was through! Step four.

He had a contact lined up, someone he'd met in the pub on Bocca. Before he went to meet him, Khadaji took his legal permit, went to a weapons supplier and bought a spetsdöd and four magazines of shocktox darts. Just in case.

There was no trouble. Ten minutes after he arrived in a

respectable clothing producer's office, Khadaji traded fifty standards worth of mescabyn for twenty-five thousand stads. He saw the money credited to his account, and he and his customer parted on the best of terms. The man would take all Khadaji could supply, he said.

Khadaji grinned as he walked toward his rented cube. He had just made more money in a few hours than in the last two years. He laughed aloud. He was tempted to spend a few days and a chunk of the money on Ago's Moon, enjoying some of the pleasures which could be had by someone well-off. But he shook the thought. No, this was only a beginning. He would have to devise other ways to make this seed grow. The switched bag caper had worked, but he wouldn't try that again. According to his research, most law benders were caught when they tried to milk too much from a good thing. He didn't plan to repeat himself and run that risk.

The term "victimless crimes" might be a misnomer, but it was one Khadaji used as his basis of operation. Smuggling seemed to him to be the best way to go. He didn't deal in killing weapons; if he smuggled drugs, they were non-addictive; he tended to buy something where it was legal and sell it where it was not. The risks he took justified his profits, in his mind, at least.

"—thing to declare, brother?"

"I bought this camera on Muta Kato," Khadaji said. "It's a gift for an old friend here."

"Looks expensive. Value, brother?"

"Four hundred standards, I'm afraid." *Not counting the flame opals hidden inside the drive motor.* "Will I have to pay an import duty?"

"That's so, sorry, brother. Fifty percent."

Khadaji pretended to wince. "Well. There goes my moth-

er's souvenir statue of His Eminence." He reached for his
credit tab.

"I'd hate to deprive somone's mother of such a gift. What
say we value this at . . . three hundred stads?"

Khadaji smiled. "You are a true saint, brother."

Khadaji kept smiling as he walked through customs. He
was glad he'd had a chance to study history; he owed an
easy twelve thousand stads to the writer of an old file called
The Purloined Letter.

When the Directorate of Simba Numa declared rec chem
An Abomination and shut down all public pubs, Khadaji
was *not* one of the chemrunners who sold a shipload of
common sops and liquids to eager buyers waving credit tags
at passing traffic. The Directorate was expecting that kind
of business and was prepared for it. Dozens of ships were
impounded and their owners and pilots arrested. Khadaji,
drawing upon his knowledge gained as a pubtender, approached a legal market selling products which could be
easily converted into various popular rec-chems and sold
them instructions on how to make those conversions. Bath-
tub psychedelics and gin became best-sellers and Khadaji
left the planet long before the authorities began looking for
him.

To cover his travel and illicit activities, Khadaji bought a
business, a firm which specialized in sending consultants
to help small businesses streamline their operations. He did
so through a series of dummy corporations and fronts, then
hired himself as a kind of free-cycle investigator, who answered only to the CEO of the company. The same CEO,
hired by Khadaji, was allowed to run the legal end of the
business as long as he vouched for Khadaji and didn't ask
him any questions.

As he made more money, Khadaji invested it in other legal operations, in stocks and banks and high-profit ventures. He wanted wealth, but it had to be useable wealth. He paid taxes on his legal earnings, hired a team of accountants to shift and juggle and obscure the input made from illegal activities, and poured the money through. The filter of respectability changed dirty stads to clean; Khadaji became solidly middle-class, then well-off, then moderately wealthy.

He put all of his energy into making money. It became a game, exciting at first because of the risks. Later, Khadaji became cautious and began paying others to take his risks for him. He worked through circular dummies, dead-end computer orders and back-check fail-safes; tracing him would be almost impossible, should his people be caught. And, on the rare occasions when one of his employees was detained, a legal fund swung into effect, along with a considerable chunk of tax-paid cash for the arrestee. Few ever willingly talked and those who did could give little away.

After almost five years, Khadaji had accomplished two things: he became known in the smuggling trade as No-Face, because no one knew who he was; and he became rich. In a galaxy where a man who was worth five million stads was someone of importance, Khadaji was as important as a dozen men. Only, nobody knew it—or him. When he met anybody not connected to his legal work, he went skin-masked; the computer worm he constructed was of such complexity that it was highly unlikely anybody could ever follow its tortuous convolutions to him from any part of his enterprises. His profile was so low as to be nearly flat, he was obsessive about keeping his identity secret. Nobody even suspected he existed, save as a well-paid flunky for a nondescript corporation; a faceless member of the business community. He had contacts of a certain kind, however, enough money to be powerful, and he had the beginnings of a plan.

SEVENTEEN ————

THERE WERE SIX human-occupied worlds in the Shin System and Renault was the least developed of the six. It was the fifth planet out from the primary G called Shin, one of the many worlds which fit the narrow slot that allowed humans to walk about and free-breathe. The gravity was a hair greater than standard single-gee, and the air a bit richer in oxygen. There were three continents, a decent axial-tilt, and something under nine million people and assorted mues living there. The main local industries were forestry and farming; primary exports to the galactic markets consisted of refined metals, although in no great amount.

Renault was another of the sidestream worlds, of little importance to the Confederation and its machinations. There was a small military outpost of a hundred troops; assignment to it was considered a form of punishment for any soldier with ambition.

Simplex-by-the-Sea was a village on the southwestern

coast of the smallest continent. The summers were hot, the winters mild and the primary industries were fishing and tourism. Civilization had brushed its technology-carrying hand past the village, but only a few seeds had fallen upon the small town. The fishing fleet had full bio-gear for locating the schools, but they still used nets; the library was nailed into the off world cast, but the scanners were antiques and subject to local weather and breakdowns. It was a place as far from Confed interest as any, and therefore perfect for Khadaji's plan.

He spent a month in the summer sunshine of Simplex-by-the-Sea and when he left, Khadaji owned a building which had once been a school for the children of the town. The last students to use the building were old enough to be grandparents; there were few children left in the village and those who were were linked to edcom at home.

Of course, the residents of Simplex-by-the-Sea, if asked, would have denied knowledge of anyone named Emile Antoon Khadaji; nor would they be able to identify the face of the man who bought the old school; for they had not seen it, in truth. But his money was good and there seemed to be plenty of it. In this town, everybody knew what everybody else did and talk was as common as the smell of fish and gulls, but one did not offend an outsider willing to spend money and maybe create jobs. The Man Who Bought the School was a hot topic after he left, but only in town. Best not to spread things too far and maybe wipe the transact, eh?

Four teams of Khadaji's agents were sent to Renault. Supplies were brought, licenses obtained—sometimes with bribes, sometimes not—and workers hired. When possible, local people were given jobs and paid much higher rates than were the union standard. The Man Who Bought the School was very popular in Simplex-by-the-Sea.

• • •

Khadaji sat in his office on Bocca. He was surrounded by handwaxed persimmon wood paneling, and the most sophisticated holoproj/comp terminal available sat on a desk of carved giant briar. A free agent didn't deserve such an office, so Khadaji had arranged to be "promoted" to a vice presidential job. He had circulated the rumor in the company that he was being kicked uplevels for inefficiency in the field, which made him someone to avoid in company political circles. Once he had the image of a loser, the other workers let him alone, just as he intended. He was getting better at manipulating people, he realized. Sometimes that bothered him, his ability to do that.

Khadaji said, "Juete," and the holoproj screen flashed the file before he could lean back in the form-chair. He smiled. She had claimed her last month's funding on Vishnu, the pleasure moon orbiting Shiva, in the Tau System. Five thousand stads were made available for her to draw each month, and the trust would last until she died. Juete would never have to work or worry about taking care of herself again. He had never actually said it was from him, but he had given Juete what—in his mind—was a strong clue as to who sent her five kay stads each month. On the original deposit, he had appended a closing salutation which read: "I understand better, now. Love, Older."

It was from a conversation they'd had early in their relationship, when she'd tried to warn him, in her own way, that she did what was necessary to take care of herself. He hadn't really understood then when she told him that with age came experience, more important than wisdom. Now he did.

Juete was never stupid; she realized immediately where the stads came from. Early on, a taped message arrived at the office of the bank administering the trust and was eventually forwarded to Khadaji's attention. It was simple enough:

"Thank you, Emile. It is you, isn't it? I see that you really did love me. If you should feel the need, I would enjoy seeing you again, to show my gratitude."

He had smiled when he'd heard the message. It contributed a small warmth to his day, even if he were less naive now than he had been when he'd met Juete. Maybe she really meant it, a pleasant thought. Or, said the cynical voice he'd developed in dealing with crooked officials and the smuggler's underground, maybe she just wanted to possess the entire goose and not just the monthly golden egg.

Well. It didn't matter. His gesture had been for him as well as for her. If she had been less truthful about telling him her needs, she could have held him forever. Truth deserved rewarding, even if it were sometimes unpleasant. Besides, if he hadn't left, he wouldn't be in a position to be generous.

"Sir?" It was the appointment voice of his comp.

"Yes?"

"Your workout is scheduled in fifteen minutes."

"Ah. So it is. Thank you."

"You are quite welcome, sir."

Khadaji stood and stretched, listening to his joints pop, feeling the play of muscle in his back and shoulders. Things were coming along nicely, but it wouldn't do for him to get out of shape. His life would depend on his conditioning.

Until the games comp was switched on, the warehouse was simply a large, empty rectangle: a stress-plastic frame and rockfoam covered building surrounding empty air. But when the computer was activated, the holographic projections made the inside of the warehouse anything it was programmed to be. A desert or a forest or a city street would spring into existence at the sound of a coded word, and the projections would look and feel almost real, courtesy of captive energies whose workings Khadaji could only partially understand.

The projections could be peopled with holoproj simulacrums, also programmed to behave as required. The machinery for generating the illusions cost over two million
standards; to his knowledge, Khadaji had the only such
device outside of military or police operations. Such toys
were considered illegal for normal game parlors.

He opened the case he carried and removed the pair of
spetsdöds. Methodically, he molded each of the weapons
onto its proper hand, then snapped loaded magazines into
place. He waved each arm experimentally, adjusting for the
slight change in weight. It was an automatic ritual now: The
dartguns made his hands feel normal; without them, he felt
bare. He walked to the center of the warehouse, to a neutral
spot which would not become part of a wall or a tree when
the comp was activated. The terrain patterns were random-
ized—he never knew which the computer would assemble
for him. Nor did he know how many spectral-but-solid
opponents the magnetic/viral bubbles would deploy.

He felt a tenseness in his back and shoulders, and he
took a deep breath and exhaled, allowing the muscles to
relax. Early on, he had warmed up before each session,
stretching and doing *kata*. He'd stopped that; in a real-life
situation, he might not have a chance to limber up and get
ready.

He took another deep breath. "Go," he said.

Reality altered. The empty warehouse became a tropical
rainforest with a snap, with no blur into apparent solidity.
Thick-leaved trees and squat bushes surrounded him, phan-
tom insects shot by emitting Doppler hums. Birds called
from the tops of the trees.

Khadaji dropped flat to the soft humus of the small clear-
ing and began to crawl rapidly toward the nearest bush.
That was a lesson he'd learned early playing these games.
He'd been "shot" several times for standing around while
trying to get his bearings in the new "world."

The jungle was noisy, but none of the sounds were those of men. No shots tore the air, no voices called for Khadaji to solidify, no detectors began screaming stridently. He grinned. Good.

He began to work his way through the bush, moving cautiously in a half-crouch, alert for any sign of trouble. Fifteen minutes later, he smelled the faint tang of gunlube. He wet a finger and held it up in the air. The wind was from *that* direction. He moved.

There were three troopers in a cleared area. One man leaned against a tree, smoking a flickstick. A woman sat on the ground, cleaning her carbine. The third man stood watch. The last man was the dangerous one, Khadaji knew that. He was a constant face, one the computer used in almost every simultation, and he was *fast*. To approximate real soldiers, the comp produced human figures with a full range of reflexes. Constant Face there sweeping the brush with his shifty gaze was the fastest of them all, superhuman in his speed, even quicker than a bacteria-augmented man. That made it unfair, but Khadaji was glad of it. If he could take Face, he should be able to take any real soldier in a one-on-one.

This was three-on-one, however, and a different matter. The theory said it was simple enough: Shoot Face with one weapon, hit the leaning man with the second and the woman would be simple; after all, her weapon was down. Face was the one to worry about.

Khadaji held very still, using the ninja-freeze techniques he'd learned. With his body control training in sumito, he could lock himself into non-motion for hours, but the ninja-freeze was even better. One practiced invisibility instead of simply being still. There was a subtle but definite difference which was not fully explained. The most common theory was that the psychological stance of being invisible helped avoid detection by anyone who might be emphatically receptive—another unproven idea.

Khadaji was waiting for Face to turn away, so he could shoot him in the back. There was no room for heroics or fair play in Khadaji's plan, the odds were already stacked in favor of the other side. Face was fast enough so he might be able to get off a shot before the simulated Spasm hit him; Khadaji didn't want to give him a target.

Finally, Face took a couple of steps and turned to look away from Khadaji's position. Leaner still leaned; the woman had her carbine only partially reassembled. Khadaji extended his arms, balancing carefully on his elbows, and fired each spetsdöd once.

Leaner doubled up fast, but Face did manage a half-spin before he knotted. He triggered a short blast of his weapon at Khadaji's position, but it was too high. If he'd been standing, the holographic shots would have tagged him. Khadaji grinned and scrambled up to finish the woman as Face dropped onto the damp ground in a fetal curl.

The woman was gone. Where—? How—?

She came from behind a tree in a dive. Khadaji swung his left spetsdöd to cover her. She hit the ground in a shoulder roll and came up facing him, five meters away. An easy shot. He fired at her solar plexus—and at the same instant, saw she held something in her hand. She threw whatever it was at him, hard.

Damn! He jumped to his right and started to sprint. It could be a proximity shrap—!

A bell chimed, a clear and insistent tone Khadaji had grown to hate. He looked down and saw a throwing steel buried in his chest. The stainless steel bar looked very real, even though he knew it was only a computer-generated image like all the rest.

Ah, damn! She got him! "Cancel it," he said, disgusted.

The throwing steel vanished abruptly, along with all of the other unreal paraphernalia produced by his two-million-stad toy. Khadaji stood alone in a bare and empty warehouse. He sighed, and shook his head. Over-confidence, that was what had done it. He'd underestimated the woman, in his concern over Face. It was a bad error; had this been real, he would be dead.

"Let's have a percentage, to date," he said. "And for the last ten sessions."

The computer's voice was bland. "Total run, seventy-eight-point-eight-six percent survival. Sessions two hundred six to two hundred sixteen, inclusive, ninety percent."

"Thanks." He was getting better, certainly. Only one "death" in the last ten runs, he'd gotten through nine out of ten, which wasn't bad in most things. It wasn't good enough, he knew. In real life, the game would be lost if he won all but one. There was no second place winner in a combat shoot, it was a pass/fail situation.

Well. He could practice his forms now and work on his unarmed combat before another run. He peeled the spets-döds away and set them aside, and began to stretch. And think.

Revolution versus evolution. The gun versus the instruction tape. Force versus peaceful means. It was no simple choice, not merely a black-or-white decision. Few things were clear-cut and this was not one of them, in his mind. To offer himself as an example of determined resistance for others to follow was one way to undermine the grasp of the Confed. To deliberately create an heroic figure to inspire and agitate by attacking with the means he despised was something he thought much about. Oh, he could rationalize it to himself by saying he was actually defending, that the Confed by its very nature forfeited its rights, in essence attacking all free people first. One was allowed to defend against attackers in Khadaji's objectivistic philosophy. The nonviolence of the strong allowed one to protect oneself as long as one did not *initiate* anything. That was reasonable.

Khadaji slid slowly down into a split, working the muscles of his legs. Despite his practice, he still could not completely stretch it out; his groin stayed clear of the floor by a good three centimeters.

Rationalization was not enough, though. He didn't feel sufficiently righteous to accept the ends-justifies-the-means easily, and the simulated troopers he was blasting had no families, friends, hopes or dreams. Real soldiers had those things. He knew. He had been a trooper. Therefore the end to justify those kinds of means had to be worthwhile, really important. Simple revolution was not enough, it left too much to chance, too many holes which would have too many people all too willing to plug them with systems worse than the Confed. So, there had to be more. And that's where it got tricky.

He bent over and tried to put his chest on the floor, still holding the split. Close.

He thought about the school he'd bought on Renault. Yes. Very tricky, indeed. So much could go wrong.

He finished the stretches and stood, then went through the six *katas* of sumito. It took almost an hour, but he felt much better when he was done. He retrieved the spetsöds and molded them into place.

"Go," he said.

The sand was green and black, and a wind stirred the desert around him. He spun quickly, looking for enemies. He didn't see any immediately, but he knew they were out there.

Waiting.

In time, his percentages of winning against the simulacrums peaked. He would, Khadaji knew, grow better still, but only by small degrees, measured in bits perhaps discernable only in theoretical, rather than practical terms. As good as the simulator was, it did lack certain things, not the least of which was real risk. To fight against the machine was one thing, to fight against living, breathing opponents was another. He considered where he could get such experience. There was the Musashi Flex, a loosely-organized band of modern ronins who travelled around challenging each other; he could try that. Or, there was The Maze. Such a thing was risky, but it offered a real test. Injury was likely, death a possibility in the game known as The Maze; if he could survive that, maybe he would be ready.

Maybe.

EIGHTEEN ——————

KHADAJI WATCHED THE three men as they moved to circle him. Two of them were larger than he, one considerably smaller. The larger men were similar only in size: One had a jagged slice on his face, probably done by a sharpened fingernail; the second had a single, thick bar of black hair where normal eyebrows would be. The last man, the shrimp, didn't seem to have much going for him. Khadaji didn't let the third man's size fool him, though; since he was still in the game, he had to have something.

Slice edged closer, looking for an opening. Brow glanced at Slice's back, but apparently decided to honor the pact, at least until Khadaji was out of the way. Shrimp was trying to get behind Khadaji, but failing, since Khadaji kept stepping slowly backward. Fortunately, this portion of The Maze was mostly empty streets, with nothing to trip a man not looking where he stepped.

Slice hurried his steps, trying to come within his own

range without entering Khadaji's defensive sphere. He was taller and so should have the reach advantage.

Khadaji considered running. After all, he didn't know how many participants were left and three-to-one odds weren't the best. There was no rule again alliances, even though the intent of the game was all-against-all. If Slice, Brow and Shrimp managed to eliminate the competition, they would have to turn against one another—there was only one winner allowed.

Brow moved closer. Khadaji kept his gaze unfocused and allowed his peripheral vision to warn him. He shifted back a hair faster, not allowing Brow to move close enough to attack without losing his center. These three were all expert in one or more martial arts, they wouldn't make any rash moves, no attack unless they were certain of success. Too much was at stake. A hundred entrants at ten thousand stads each, winner take all—the winner being the last man or woman standing—or breathing.

Shrimp darted by Khadaji quickly, at a run. If Khadaji was going to take off, it would have to be now. He grinned, and stopped moving suddenly. No. He didn't need the money, but he had to know that he could win against real opponents rather than computer simulations, no matter how sophisticated the machine. A loss here was worth serious and real injury, maybe even death. Despite the latest in medical gear standing by, Maze gamers had been known to die.

Slice made the first move. He squared his stance into a riding horse variant and looked at Khadaji over his left shoulder and raised fist. Since he was a big man and powerful, Khadaji figured him for a strength attack, maybe a kick—

It came. Slice cross-stepped and threw a sidekick, his heel aiming for Khadaji's groin. Well. At least he had sense enough not to kick high, like some holoproj artist. Khadaji sidestepped and used both hands to increase the speed of Slice's thrust. It overbalanced the man's weight on his ground foot and Slice fell heavily onto his side—

Brow leaped in, trying to catch Khadaji off guard. Brow shot a stiffened hand at Khadaji's throat, his fingers bunched into a spear—

Khadaji spun away from the strike. He grinned as he found himself following the pattern of steps Pen had made him learn so many years ago. He had time to remember the numbers, seventy-one and two, then he extended his own hands and caught Brow's wrist. Continuing his turn, Khadaji levered Brow into a fall and the man became an eighty-five kilo missile with a bone-tipped warhead—landing right onto Slice as the first man tired to scramble up. There was a *clunk!* of Brow's skull hitting Slice's face. Slice was down again and unconscious; Brow was stunned. Khadaji spun on the balls of his feet to face Shrimp, who aborted his own attack and came to a stop. Shrimp regarded Slice and Brow, then looked back at Khadaji, whose stance was neutral and relaxed.

"Truce?" Shrimp said. "You and I, we can finish them and work together. There are maybe six or eight others left. After that. . . ."

"No," Khadaji said. "I play alone."

Shrimp appeared to be weighing his chances of fighting or running. Behind him, Khadaji heard Brow groan, then collapse. A telemetric scanner whined from above The Maze, and Khadaji knew both men were out of the game. A medical din would be coming for them soon.

Abruptly, Shrimp decided. He turned and ran.

Six or eight left, he'd said. Khadaji had figured more, so he must have missed a couple of the telemetric signals, that was bad. Unless Shrimp had been wrong. But he'd looked shrewd, that one, and Khadaji wondered again what skill had kept him in the game this far. They were three days into The Maze, a holoprojic construct built especially for such things. If only eight or ten players remained, it would likely be over soon. Some were no doubt hiding, hoping the others would take each other out, but they would have to emerge sooner or later. There was a time limit of a week; if more than one person remained on the field by then, the game was voided. It was not enough merely to survive; one had to survive alone. . . .

Khadaji found himself walking down a wide street flanked by holoprojic buildings programmed to look like a heavy industrial district. Plenty of places to hide, doorways, alleys, refuse containers.

Suddenly there was a blur of motion half a block ahead. Khadaji slid behind the cover of a metal container and cautiously stuck his head around the edge to see what was happening.

It was a skirmish. A tall woman with dusky skin faced a shorter man built like a powerlifter. They circled, hands held in defensive postures.

Khadaji cautiously moved closer, keeping to the shadowy doorways, being careful not to allow his attention on the fighters distract his check for hidden players. He stopped twenty meters away from the pair and watched.

Unless the woman was very skilled, Khadaji would put his money on the powerlifter. The man moved well and was obviously very strong. If he managed to close with the woman, she would be in trouble.

The two feinted a few times, the woman giving ground. The powerlifter might be certain he could take her, but he was not stupid; that the woman had managed to survive where so many others had not was obviously in his mind.

Eventually, the powerlifter backed the woman into a corner, between a grimy wall and a rack of heavy machinery. He gathered himself, and lunged at her, hands open wide to grab her—

The woman was skilled. She threw half a dozen punches and kicks, sharp and powerful attacks. She scored; the powerlifter was hurt, but he kept coming. He locked his arms around her and lifted her free of the ground in a bear hug—

She continued to lance at him, but he ducked his head into her and kept squeezing. She was a wasp, stinging a gorilla. Khadaji heard ribs snap—

The woman put the tip of her little finger into her mouth and bit down, hard. Khadaji frowned. What—?

She pulled her finger from her mouth and spat the tip of it into her palm, then turned her hand over and slapped it onto the top of the powerlifter's head. There was cracking sound and the powerlifter suddenly collapsed, releasing the woman.

A telemetric siren began to scream and the voice of a medical din blared at the combatants in a metallic clang: "Ordnance foul! Ordnance foul! Ordnance foul!"

The woman turned to run, but was quickly surrounded by four dins waving prods. While the medical din continued to repeat the foul charge, Khadaji turned and hurried away. All the commotion was as apt to drive players away as draw them. The woman had cheated, she had somehow gotten a weapon past the scanners. Must have been some organic explosive charge, Khadaji figured, shaped to blast hard enough to fry a human or mutant brain. The powerlifter was likely dead; the woman would be disqualified and penalized. Two more players gone.

Feeding stations were prime places for attacks. Khadaji had avoided them as much as possible for that reason. He waited until "night," watched a station for at least an hour before moving on it, and was in and out quickly. Many of the players were taken at meal times as they sauntered into some carefully-set trap placed by expert hunters. Like water holes in some primitive jungle, the feeding stations in The Maze were dangerous, no less so because all the users were predators *and* prey.

Khadaji was on the roof of a structure overlooking one of the ten stations. It was near midnight and he had been lying there for nearly two hours, watching and listening. Normally, he would have moved in long before, but something had made a noise thirty minutes into his watch, and he had not yet been able to pinpoint the source. He was hungry and thirsty, but this only made his hypnotically trained senses sharper. He hoped.

Just as he was preparing to give up the watch as an overcautious worry, a man appeared from a pile of refuse cans and cat-footed toward the food dispensers. Ah, there had been something. Funny, it had seemed to come from a closer source, but sounds did strange things in such surroundings. He watched the man.

As the figure reached a spot two meters from the dispensers, there was a flurry of additional motion. A second man appeared—Khadaji couldn't tell where from, exactly—and a short fight ensued. The second man was vicious; he clubbed the first from behind with his hands locked together, hitting him repeatedly at the base of the skull. After the man was down, the attacker continued to hit him, until the drone of the robot dins bringing medical gear grew close.

On the roof, Khadaji suddenly felt sick. This game wasn't only a game. Sure, the man would likely survive his assault; sure, he had known the risks, had wanted the money enough to take them. But it was like watching two animals—

A voice took over the night. "According to the rules of

The Maze Game, we are required to inform you that two contestants remain at an elapsed time of five days, nine hours, forty minutes, twelve seconds."

Khadaji took a deep breath. His sumito, his art of personal control, allowed him much leeway, and he didn't do what the attacker below had done. He turned the force of an attack upon itself, he *defended*, using the energy of another against himself. Or herself. But in the now-quiet darkness, he shook his head.

Am I any better than that man down there? Isn't violence violence, no matter how it is wrapped with clever rationalization? The others have destroyed each other for money and I have a higher goal: freedom from the yoke of the Confederation. But at what price? These players were all people, with families, and friends and lives they wished to live, weren't they?

Gods, is what I'm doing right? *Can I really justify it?*

Khadaji watched as the dins removed the downed man. The winner of the fight moved into a patch of pale blue light cast by the food dispensers. Khadaji recognized him: Shrimp.

Is what I'm doing right? Even at such cost? Once I was certain, I had that knowledge, *now I am not so sure, not so sure at all. But I spent a big portion of my life so far working toward it. Can I quit now?*

No. No, he decided, you can't. It might cost you personally, but if you reach your goal, it will be worth it. It has to be worth it.

"You might as well come out," Khadaji said. "I know where you are and there are only two of us left, now." He stood facing the dispensers, five meters back.

After a moment, Shrimp appeared. This time, Khadaji saw his hiding place, a cleverly built arrangement which folded against the wall. At night, in the dark, it would be hard to see until one was nearly upon it.

"I thought you might make it," Shrimp said. "I've seen that stuff you did before. Some kind of religious fighting style, isn't it? I didn't think anybody as good as you are at it would be interested in playing in The Maze, though."

"I'm not, really," Khadaji said. "I've got other reasons. I don't need the money."

"Oh? Why not default then, and let me have it?" Shrimp edged a hair closer to Khadaji.

"I would. Except I don't think you deserve it."

"Ah, but I *do* deserve it, you see. I've won this game before. Came in second twice. It isn't the money."

Khadaji nodded. "You like it. The hurting. The fighting."

Shrimp moved to his right, so the light fell more upon him. "Oh, yeah. You have to, to win."

Khadaji shook his head. "No, you don't. If you've got enough reason, you can hate it and win."

Shrimp held his hands up in front of his chest and brought them slowly together. "You jest, friend. You might fool somebody else with the philosophical rat shit, but it's just you and me and we know what we are, don't we?" He brought his hands together suddenly and began a finger weave. Shrimp's fingers danced in the pale light, knotting and unknotting in intricate and complex patterns designed to draw a watcher into them. It was a variation on classical kuji-kiri called *Neshomezoygn,* and he was very good. But Khadaji had first seen the organomechanical hypnosis years ago, when Pen had used it to beat him in their first encounter; he had learned how to use it—and avoid being taken by it since. Now he knew too how Shrimp had survived The Maze. But it wasn't going to be enough, this time.

Khadaji stepped in toward the other man.

A moment later, there was a new winner of The Maze

Game. And a new loser. As Khadaji stared at the unconscious form of the man he'd thought of as Shrimp, he knew
the winner and loser were, in fact, the same. But at least
he knew also that he was as ready as he was likely to be
to begin the next step in his plan.

The thrum of the dins surrounded him as he stood there
nodding slowly to himself. Yes. He was ready.

NINETEEN

HE ARRANGED FOR competent people to take care of his business and money. That was easy enough, since he already had most of them in place. Then Khadaji took passage on a ship and was bent through half a galaxy to a world with enough strategic importance to rate recent occupation by ten thousand members of the Confederation ground forces.

Fourteen years after and billions of kilometers away from the Slaughter on Maro, Emile Antoon Khadaji arrived on Greaves.

The old man's name was Hinton, and aside from his age and the fact that he owned the pub, he had a kind of cackle which reminded Khadaji of Kamus. Hinton was tired. He had run the rec-chem operation for thirty local years and whatever joy it might have once held for him had long since fled. Khadaji's agents had supplied him with information about Hinton and the Jade Flower, as well as three similar operations, so it was no surprise to Khadaji.

Of the places carefully investigated, the Jade Flower was first choice. The only problem he saw in buying it was the price. Not that he couldn't afford it—ninety million standards would buy most of the town—but he had to be careful to offer enough and not too much. The old boy might wonder about that, and what Khadaji didn't want at this stage was any suspicion from anybody. But, since Khadaji knew precisely what the pub was worth, he had an advantage.

They sat in Hinton's office, the old man behind a plastic desk and Khadaji in a worn form-chair which kept slipping a gear and poking him in the left buttock.

"My partners and I are willing to offer a hundred and fifty kay," Khadaji said. That was low, by fifteen percent. The place was worth st172,500, according to Khadaji's people.

"Not a chance," Hinton said. "I might accept two hundred, but I'd be cheating myself."

Khadaji kept a straight face. "Well. I might be able to get my partners to go to a hundred and sixty."

"And let an old man starve? Shee-it."

Khadaji would have paid ten times what the place was worth, but it was important the old man not think so. After a few minutes of bargaining, and a fake call to his "partners," Khadaji allowed himself to be talked up to a final price of 190,000 stads. He was pleased, the old man was pleased, and the Jade Flower was Khadaji's.

The detail man from the chem distribution outfit was surprised, but didn't let that temper his greed.

"Full spectrum? How deep are we talking here?"

Khadaji allowed himself a small grin. "I'm planning on a good business. We already have military on-limits status and I—my partners and I—plan to go full day and night cycle."

The man nodded, and Khadaji could almost see his mind

adding up his percentage of the new order. According to
Hinton's records, the Jade Flower was a break-even proposition most of the time. With a full-spectrum order for
rec-chem, the detail man's commission would jump considerably. He smiled broadly, and waved his portable trans-
ducer at the holoproj. "Well, I suggest a basic order along
these lines. . . ."

Khadaji smiled and nodded. The man was adding twenty
percent to what was really needed. Khadaji let him finish,
then cut the order by ten percent. That showed he wasn't
a fool, but still allowed the detail man enough skim to make
him happy.

"Lemme see I got this right," the constructor said. "You
wanna buy the round tables with a quad set of stools, but
you wanna have 'em bolted to the floor?"

"That's right," Khadaji said. They stood in the center of
the Jade Flower's octagon room, amidst the bulky long
tables Hinton was currently using.

The constructor nodded. "No problem. What—ah—you
gonna do with the—old furnishings?"

"I thought I'd sell them."

"I—ah—can make you an offer."

Khadaji raised an eyebrow.

The constructor looked at him for a moment, then named
a figure which was half the value of the old tables and
benches. Khadaji nodded in return, then made a counter-
offer. In the end, he allowed the constructor to take the old
furniture for enough so the man would make a nice profit
when he resold them.

He didn't fire any of the people Hinton had working for
him; he didn't want any ex-employees causing problems.
With the expanded scope of operations, more help would

be needed. Khadaji contacted an employment service with his needs.

Anjue Yesmar Levart was a thin, dark, intense native of Spandle. He used his hands when he spoke, weaving a picture around his words. Khadaji detected in Anjue the qualities he wanted in a doorman. He seemed quick, had a good memory and ten years of experience. Khadaji ran six of the constructor's helpers past each applicant for the job, and Anjue recalled all their names after one introduction. More, Anjue remember what they were wearing before he saw them again. And he was polite but not obsequious. Khadaji hired him and gave him leave to hire his own assistant.

Hiring a head pubtender was relatively easy. With his own background, Khadaji knew which questions to ask. Of the first half dozen applicants the agency sent over, only one knew the ingredients to Shin's Kiss. Samar "Butch" Beavens knew not only a Shin's Kiss, but also every drink Khadaji asked about, and obviously a lot more he didn't know. Khadaji gave him the job and told him to hire assistants as needed. Butch would take care of selecting prostitutes, as well.

The man was burly, but not too bright. He stared at Khadaji. They were alone in the octagon, in the middle of the newly-installed round tables and stools. Khadaji repeated it. "I want you to pick up a stool. Be careful, they are bolted to the floor."

The man digested that, shrugged, and stepped to the stool nearest him. He leaned over and gripped the stool, bending at the waist. He took a deep breath and gathered himself—

"Hold it," Khadaji said. "That's enough."

"Huh?"

"I'll contact the agency and they'll let you know."

It took a while for that to filter through, but finally the man nodded and turned to leave. Khadaji tapped a key and crossed the man's name from the computer's file. Anybody who used his lower back in lifting, as he'd been about to do, didn't know the right way to utilize his muscles. Besides, he hadn't walked like a man who knew how to move well. Khadaji had Anjue bring in the next one.

The next applicant came across the floor as if he owned it. He moved in balance, a point in his favor. Khadaji looked at the file and saw that the man called himself Sleel. According to the application, he had several years training in tahrae, a form of jujitsu.

"Sleel. That a last name?"

"It's what I go by."

Khadaji nodded. Sleel didn't look particularly muscular under his two-piece, though he did have fairly wide shoulders. "The stools are bolted to the floor," he said. "I want to see how strong the bolts are. See if you can move one."

"Sure." Sleel untabbed his tunic and slipped it off, and Khadaji revised his opinion upward. Sleel had muscle. He wasn't all that broad, but he looked thick and dense and he carried no fat.

Sleel touched a stool, tried to wiggle it, then bent and looked at the base. He walked around the stool, then planted his feet to the sides, squatted, and kept his back straight as he gripped the cross bars under the seat. He took a deep breath and tried to straighten. Ten seconds passed. Tortuous veins stood out on Sleel's muscles like tiny hoses under great pressure. The muscles of his neck and back and shoulders showed cross-striations; his whole upper body turned red. Suddenly, Sleel relaxed, took another grip, and repeated the lift. He did it three more times, long after most men would have quit, Khadaji thought. Khadaji started to stop him, but Sleel put a final effort into his war against the stool, and the bolts gave up the fight. The stool came out of the floor with a *grinch!* of metal tearing. Sleel stood there for a second, holding the stool, before he set it carefully atop one of the tables. He turned back toward Khadaji. "Anything else?"

Khadaji could feel Sleel's arrogance, his total confidence in himself. He grinned. "We open in a week," he said. "Can you start then? Butch will discuss your schedule and pay."

Sleel grinned back at Khadaji. "You got it."

The next twelve men and two women failed to budge one of the bolted stools. Then Bork came in. Saval Bork, according to the file, and he was a large man. Khadaji figured his height at near two meters and his weight at a hundred and twenty or twenty-five kilos. The man reminded him of a bear he had seen in a zoo, once. Only Bork didn't lumber, he walked with such a deliberate step he looked absolutely unstoppable.

Khadaji said. "I want you to move a stool for me. That one." Khadaji pointed at the one nearest Bork.

"Yes sir," Bork said. He reached with his right hand and grabbed the stool by the cross bar.

Khadaji started to warn Bork that the stool was bolted to the floor, but he saw the big man pause as he realized something was holding the stool down. The pause was no more than a second. Then Bork straightened. Khadaji saw the muscles of Bork's upper back work under his coverall, heard the big man grunt, and the stool came free. He'd done with one hand what more than a dozen others had failed to do with two.

"Where would you like it?" Bork asked.

"Anywhere. Can you start work in a week?"

• • •

Twenty-nine people had applied for jobs as bouncers and so far, Khadaji only had two. He needed three.

Dirisha Zuri was a tall black woman with green eyes. As Khadaji watched her walk across the floor toward him, he was more impressed with her than any of the other applicants. She wore a blue body stocking under ruffles, and she moved with perfect control. Her file said she had trained in at least four different close combat styles, and of all those he'd interviewed, Khadaji knew immediately she was the most adept in that arena. She had the job before she got to where he stood. But he wanted to see how she would handle the test.

Dirisha touched the stool lightly with her fingers, then stepped away from it. She pushed at the base with one foot. She bent and looked under the table nearest the stool. She stood, and stepped up to the table. She locked both hands onto one edge of the table's top, took several deep breaths, then set herself. She screamed, a low guttural yell, and yanked the top of the heavy plastic table free of its base. She turned and smiled at Khadaji, then used the table top like a hammer against the nearest stool. It took five shots before the stool tore free, sheared from the bolts. She set the table top back onto its base. "You said move it," she said. "It is moved."

Khadaji laughed. "And you're hired."

The constructor was puzzled and a little upset. "What happened?"

"A little test for my bouncers," Khadaji said. "I want you to use longer and stronger bolts when you fix them. And replace all the other bolts, too. I don't want my customers bashing each other with my furniture, should they become agitated." No, that wouldn't do, to be declared off-limits by the military. He needed to have their business, it was essential to his plan. The Jade Flower was going to be popular and quiet, the kind of place a trooper could go and relax and not worry about fighting. Fighting was not going to be allowed. Sleel, Bork and Dirisha would see to that.

"It's gonna take a couple of days."

"Put a rush on it. I want to open in a week. How is the drugstore room coming?"

"Nearly done. I got techs setting the densecris tomorrow and a smith installing the reaper locks this afternoon. It'll be done inna few days."

"Good."

Khadaji went to his office. So far, everything had gone well, at least physically. There was still the other, the mental part of it. The plan was working, but he still had his doubts as to whether it should ever have been started. He had his sense of mission, that was strong. And he had the haunting memory of Maro, that would never go away. And, too, there was his Realization, his lightning moment. It was time-faded, but he could remember the sense of rightness he'd felt after it. He had those things. Still, there was a schism between the thought and the deed. Theory and practice were separated by a gulf not easily crossed. Killing sentient beings was wrong; massive killing on a scale done by the Confed to maintain its warped existence was more wrong. The Confed was evil and dying, but its death had to be hastened, to avoid more senseless murder. What he would do here on Greaves, if he were successful, would speed up the fall. One man could make a difference and that would give millions of men hope. The Confed could be resisted. But that was only a part of it. There was more, greater in importance. Revolution and evolution, brothers of a different speed, but brothers nonetheless. The galaxy would see one thing happening here, but there would be something else unseen happening, as well. *If* he could pull it off. Only thing was, he would have to hurt people to do it. Not kill them, not if he could help it, but certainly he would cause them pain, stealing a part of their lives. That was not an easy thing to think about. Not at all.

TWENTY

THERE WAS THE matter of obtaining weapons. The choice was, of course, spetsdöds. Khadaji could have easily bought enough of the hand weapons to outfit his own army, but the form was important. It was necessary that spetsdöds come from the Confed forces; further, they would have to be stolen, not bought from someone looking for a fast stad. Spetsdöds were of limited use in the military, utilized mostly by prison guards, and by security personnel where deadlier weapons might be dangerous, such as in a fragile *in vitro* lab. Finding out low-level information such as nonlethal weapons shipments was relatively easy with the sophisticated computer gear Khadaji had. Stealing the weapons themselves was somewhat more difficult.

The warehouse was standard Confed construction; expanded hardfoam with plastic doors. Guards had been mounted near the loading bay and main entrance, with additional patrols

covering the emergency exits. Eight troopers altogether.
They tended to stick close to the pools of light cast by the
HT lamps on each corner of the building. It was sloppy of
them, but then, there had been no trouble on Greaves in the
months they'd been on planet. Besides there was nothing
really valuable or dangerous in the warehouse. It was mostly
full of uniforms, paper supplies and miscellaneous material.
And, Khadaji knew, several cases of small arms, including
spetsdöds.

Getting inside would be the hard part. He didn't want
trouble until he had what he wanted; therefore, he had to
bypass the guards and the alarm system designed to prevent
pilferage. Going through a door or a wall was out, digging
under would take too long; therefore, he would go in through
the roof.

He chose a rainy night, when clouds blocked all natural
skylight. The rain was cold and steady, and it kept the guards
huddled under any shelter they could find near the building.
Patrols were done, but reluctantly and quickly.

Khadaji lay in the wet darkness, and watched two troopers hurry past his position. Their voices were almost lost in
the sound of water flowing from buildings through gutters
and onto the drenched ground.

"—fucking detail ain't worth shit—!"

"—a leak in my suit, my leg is getting wet—"

As soon as they passed, Khadaji moved. He scrambled
up and ran to stand next to the building. He took a synlon
ladder from his backpack and unrolled it carefully. He removed the cover from two blocks of sticktite and squeezed
each clump of the soft plastic substance to activate the
chemicals within, then carefully allowed the end of the
ladder attached to the sticktite to hang by his side. In a few
seconds, the blocks of sticktite would adhere to anything
with a specific gravity greater than water; they would not
let go unless a special solvent was used and then only re-

luctantly. Still moving carefully, Khadaji swung the synlon chord back and forth like a pendulum. With a final swing, he tossed the weighted end up. The ladder arced over the edge of the roof. The sticktite nailed itself down and became a part of the hardfoam roof, as solid as a rock.

Khadaji clambered up the ladder and cleared the edge of the roof. He pulled the ladder up behind him and pressed himself flat. The angle was slight, just enough so water would run off easily, but even so, the wet surface was slippery. It would not do to fall five meters to the ground, he thought.

He pulled a small tremor knife from his belt and cut a circle the size of his hand through the hardfoam. He slipped the spookeyes he wore on his forehead down and clicked them on. The inside of the warehouse lit up in ghostly green. He saw a collection of trash boxes a few meters away. Good. He slapped a patch over the hole he'd cut and moved along the roof. He slipped once, but caught himself before sliding far. About where he saw the trash, Khadaji cut another hand-sized hole. Ah, yes, he was right over it. He took an electronic confounder from his pack. There was a thin line attached to the device. Khadaji used the line to lower the confounder until it was hidden among the trash boxes below. He cut the line. Then he patched the second hole and pulled a remote transmitter from his pack. "Sorry to disturb your sleep, troops." He thumbed a control on the unit. Intruder alarms began screaming.

The building vibrated under him as the doors were opened and the guards ran in. Light would be flaring inside, he knew, and the watch officer would be getting a com call from the guards. Something had set off the proximity alarms in warehouse seven, something bigger than a rat and on the floor.

The search took about thirty minutes. Since the troopers were looking for an intruder and not an electronic box hidden in the trash, they didn't find either. He could hear them through the thin patch as they searched.

"—bad circuit is all, you think, Hal—?"

"—could get in here, the doors are all sealed—"

"—least get out of the fucking rain for a while—"

"—empty as my credit tab—"

Khadaji switched the transmitter off—it was a line-of-sight maser and so would be almost impossible for a sweeper to pick up, unless he was directly over it—and the alarms died.

He waited another fifteen minutes and then switched on the confounder. The alarms blared into noisy life again.

The search was repeated. Khadaji killed his transmitter and the confounder.

Ten minutes later, he turned them back on once more.

This time, he heard the trooper in charge of the guards yelling into his com. "Shut it down! There isn't anybody here, we have fucking looked three fucking times! Maybe the fucking rain has shorted some fucking circuit out somefuckingwhere. I don't care. Get a tech over here. What? That's not my fault, you spread them out that way. How long? An hour? Fine. Nobody is gonna walk off with the fucking place. We'll be outside like good little soldiers, protecting the fuck out of all this valuable stow. Yeah, yeah, right. Discom." Then, a moment later, "Fucking asshole!"

When Khadaji tried the confounder the fourth time, no alarm answered. He grinned. Good thing, he was getting cold, despite the orthoskins. He pulled the tremor knife from his belt.

It took ten minutes to find the spetsdöds, another three to load twenty of them and ten thousand rounds of ammunition into his pack. Less the two he strapped on, with magazines of Spasm for each. He climbed the boxes he'd stacked to the roof and left through the hole he'd cut. The rain was going to make a mess of whatever was under the hole, but that was one more blow for the Shamba Freedom Forces against the Confed.

He left the synlin ladder hanging from the roof and scuttled away into the rainy night. Maybe he should have picked off a couple of the troopers, but he figured they would have enough trouble as soon as the theft was discovered. Besides, he was still reluctant to start. He had the spetsdöds and ammo, that ought to be enough for one night.

It was almost a week before he shot his first troopers, a quad he'd seen at his pub hours earlier. They were all stoned and it was no challenge. He hit them in the back; it wasn't sporting, but then again, it wasn't supposed to be. It was war.

And so the months on Greaves passed, with the Shamba Scum laying waste to the Confederation's finest. They grew in number, the Scum, according to the dispatches Khadaji tapped into. There was more than a little concern in official circles.

Gradually, Khadaji came to accept what he was doing, to a degree. It still bothered him when he thought about it; only, he didn't think about it much any more. It became his job and he tried to stay dispassionate. But he had nightmares at times, not always triggered by drug use. It had to be done, what he did, but he took no joy in it.

Eventually, as all things do, Khadaji's plan wound its way toward a climax.

Finally, they knew who he was.

Finally, they came for him.

TWENTY-ONE ————

AND SO HERE he was. Sitting on the floor of a drug vault, waiting for the Confed to come and extract its revenge. They wanted him alive, of course, but that wasn't going to happen. It would spoil all the months of work, make it all worth so much less. Oh, sure, what he'd done would still be remarkable, but it would be less than perfect. And once they had him, they could make him say or do anything, eventually. He had no illusions about that. They could peel his brain like an onion.

Well. So much for quiet meditation. He touched upon his past in the last few moments, had brought forth the good and the bad, some of the people he had known and loved. He was, he supposed, as ready as he would ever be.

There were a couple of things left to do, before the troopers arrived. He looked at a package gathering dust in the corner and smiled. It had been there since the beginning, over six months. Khadaji took a few steps and picked up

the package, a plastic box sealed with security strips. It was
heavier than he remembered. Or, maybe he was just tired—

"—looking for the owner, Khadaji!"

The transceiver over the window picked up the voice of
the trooper clearly. Khadaji smiled. So. At last. They were
here. He stepped in front of the densecris window and touched
a control, depolarizing the crystal to clarity once again.
There were a dozen troopers crowding into the room, all
wearing class three armor and waving carbines. One soldier
carried a grenade launcher. Khadaji smiled more broadly
and felt himself become calm. It was the waiting that was
hard, not the doing. He waved at the troopers. "Here I am,"
he said. Then he touched the control for the densecris and
the window faded to black.

"Open it!" the Lojtnant said, waving his sidearm at Butch.

"I can't. It can only be opened from the inside."

Sleel stepped forward. "What's the scat, Lojt?"

"I want that man."

"Why?"

The Lojt turned on Sleel. "Who the hell are you?"

"I'm the man who is going to flatten you if you don't
come up with some reasons for being here."

The Lojt laughed. He was pointing a rocket pistol at
Sleel's belly; more, he was dressed in class three armor,
which was proof against any weapon in the room, save the
grenade launcher. Even so, he shouldn't have laughed.

Sleel stepped forward and hooked his right heel behind
the Lojt's ankle, then shoved against the man's chest, hard.
The Lojt went down, flat onto his back. He looked like a
giant beetle as he waved his arms and legs, trying to right
himself. There was a procedure, but he wasn't using it.

Sleel smiled, but the smile vanished when a trooper
thunked his carbine's butt into the back of Sleel's head. He

fell. Butch dropped to his knees and cradled the fallen man's head.

Three troopers helped the Lojtnant to his feet. Behind the faceplate of his armor, the man's face was livid. "Get that door open!"

Two men waddled toward the door in their armor. One began kicking it while the other slammed his carbine's stock against the handle.

From the floor, Butch said, "I wouldn't do that. There are reaper locks installed there."

The door's alarm system began squalling, a singsong *whoop-whoop*. A recorded voice began blasting the two troopers: "WARNING, REAPER SEQUENCE ENACTED. STAND CLEAR. WARNING, REAPER SEQUENCE ENACTED—"

The two troopers looked at the Lojt, who waved the rocket pistol at the door. "Go on!"

The recorded voice warned them a final time. Then the reapers went off. Four finger-thick steel bars shot out of the door, two each near the upper left and lower right sides, angled across the door. The two troopers weren't hit, but before they could move, the steel rods whipped out from the bars. The top set took the men at shoulder height; the bottom set just below the knees. An unarmored man would have been broken in half; as it was, the troopers were flipped sideways as if they were toys. The reapers re-cocked themselves.

"Damn!"

"I told you," Butch said.

"Back off!" The Lojt yelled. He pointed his rocket pistol at the door and triggered it. The rocket reached the sound barrier just before it hit the door; there was a double boom. A burn scar flashed the steel, but the door held firm.

"All civilians out!"

When the room was clear of everybody but his men, the

Lojt said, "Take out the window."

A tall woman raised her Parker and let loose a blast. The densecris shook under the impact of the explosive slugs, but didn't crack. It didn't even star. There was a line of black spotches, no more.

"God*damn!*" The Lojt was so angry he shook. "Listen up in there, mister! You come out, now, or we're going to implode the damned room, you copy that?"

There was no answer.

"Outside, everybody but the L-45!"

One of the Sub-Lojts said, "Sir, aren't we supposed to capture—?"

"I said *out!*"

The troopers cleared the room, fast. In a minute, only the Lojt and the trooper carrying the L-45 were left standing in the doorway. "Blow it," the Lojt said. He was grinning like a man on the wrong side of sanity.

"Not from in here," the soldier said. "It's liable to suck us in when it goes."

"Blow it!"

The trooper looked at the Lojt's face and decided disobeying him was a bigger risk. He raised the L-45 and pointed it at the sheet of densecris. He took a deep breath, held it, then fired.

The grenade hit the window and there came that muffled *whuff!* of an impolsion device. Objects not tied down leaped at the sudden vacuum. The trooper with the L-45 was already scrambling backwards and he cleared the door. The Lojt stood like a rock, leaning against the wind. There was a bright flash of red light, going to blue, and a sonic blast which shattered glass for a kilometer around. Things got very quiet.

In the wreckage of what had been the Jade Flower, the drug vault and all its contents compacted into a sphere three meters around. Much of the space around the atomic particles which made up the seemingly solid material was eliminated. The ball sank through the pub like lead through feathers, until it buried itself deeply in the earth below.

Behind the faceplate of his armor, the Lojtnant was still smiling tightly. He didn't know it, but the war on Greaves had just ended.

For now.

TWENTY-TWO ————

IT WAS, THE OB thought, a good thing Creg was laid away with Spasm poisoning; otherwise he'd wish he were. As it stood, the Senior Sub, a whipcord woman named Pease, was hearing most of what Creg would have heard.

"—inept management I've ever seen!" Over-Befalhavare Venture said. He paused for a breath.

Pease jumped in before the OB could take off again. "Sir, this man Khadaji, the leader of the resistance, was very resourceful. He *was* a Jumptrooper—"

"—a decade and a half ago," the OB said. "Where was he between the time he deserted on—" he looked at the HX on the holoproj's imager, "—Maro and his arrival on this backrocket dinge of a world?"

Pease took a breath, but the question was rhetorical. The OB continued. "Creg never would have caught him if he hadn't sauntered into this very office and *told* him who he was."

"The attacks on our troops have stopped," Pease tried. "The death of their leader—"

"Sub-Befalhavare Pease, I know you heard the recording this man Khadaji left. Did it occur to you the reason the attacks have stopped might just be because what he said was true? That maybe he *was* the resistance—alone?"

The woman stood at parade rest, as formal a position as full attention, despite the term. She looked pale, but determined when she spoke. "Impossible, sir. The logistics of the attacks, the sheer numbers preclude that. He was lying."

The OB nodded, as if to himself. Yes. He had seen the numbers. It didn't seem likely, even if possible, that one man could have done so much damage. Word of the resistance to Confederation forces on Greaves had spread to other worlds, of course, and was damaging enough when it was thought that hundreds or thousands were responsible. If it were even suspected that a single man could do such... well, that was not a pleasant thought, not at all.

Venture looked at the holoproj again. "So, in the two weeks since Khadaji was imploded, there have been no attacks on our troops whatsoever?"

Pease allowed herself a small smile. "None, sir."

"And we are certain this pub owner is dead?"

Pease nodded at the computer. "The chemist's report is in the files, sir. With an implosion device, the only way to be sure a human was included in the condensation is a deep-spec analysis of the material. The breakdown indicates the constituents of a human body were present, within normal parameters, and allowing for error due to compressed mass."

Over-Befalhavare Venture nodded. That much was good, anyway.

The intercom came to life.

"Yes?"

"Sir, we have a report on the rebel leader."

"Well, stick it into the computer."

There was a slight pause, then the Lojt said, "I—ah—don't think that would be—ah—wise, sir. We in MI think it should be classed A1A—ah—pending your approval, of course. Sir."

Venture sighed. A1A. Top Secret, Eyes Only for Full-Clearance Personnel. Damn. Now what? "All right. Bring it in."

The door slid aside and a starch-spined Lojt marched in, carrying a small reader. He handed it to the OB and stood back at attention. Venture stared at the reader. "All right, Lojtnant, what am I about to look at?"

"Sir, this is a report on the inventory taken of the rebel Khadaji's personal effects."

Over-Befalhavare Venture stared at the young officer sourly. "Son, I have a lot on my mind. Why don't you tell me precisely why MI thinks how many pairs of socks and tunics this man had is important enough to make A1A noises over."

The Lojtnant swallowed and took a deep breath. "Sir, if the Systems Marshal will punch up code A-slash-S-slash-D, I think the answer will present itself."

Venture glared at the man. "It had better, Lojtnant." He tapped in the code. The inducer in the desk's computer picked up the signal from the reader and put the file on-screen. The military jargon was there, but it had been fifty years since it had caused Venture any problems. At eighty, he might be a bit past his prime, but he was still sharp.

FLECHETTES / ANTI-PERSONNEL / SPASM / SPETSDÖD

BOXES / 25   TOTAL ROUNDS / 7500

UNBOXED MAGAZINES, COMPLETE / 9 TOTAL ROUNDS / 108

UNBOXED MAGAZINES, PARTIAL / 1 TOTAL ROUNDS / 04

INVENTORY TOTAL / 7612

The OB looked up from the read at the Lojt. "I am impressed. MI knows how to count—obviously the canard about 'Military' and 'Intelligence' is not an example of oxymora, after all. Is there a point to this, Lojtnant?"

The younger man seemed to sag a little from his stiff posture, without any movement the OB could detect. He said, "Sir, the Spasm darts in Khadaji's possession, along with fourteen gas-operated fully automatic dorsal hand weapons—spetsdöds—were stolen from an arms shipment to this base seven-and-a-half months ago. Twenty spetsdöds and ten thousand rounds of ammunition, to be precise."

"So he was shooting our men with our weapons. Not uncommon during guerrilla warfare, son. The point?"

The man sighed and swallowed again. "Sir, if I might beg the Systems Marshal's indulgence a moment longer, please add file T-slash-W-slash-S to the screen."

Venture shook his head. "Why is it I get the impression you're trying to get *me* to say the horse is dead, Lojtnant?"

The Lojt was silent, and the OB shook his head again and punched in the second code. Another jumble of military acronymity lit the air, and Venture scrolled to the basic data enshrouded in the tangle.

CONFEDERATION TROOPERS HOSPITALIZED FOR CONTRACTURE POISONING, TOTAL / 2388.

Venture looked up. The Lojt didn't wait for permission to speak. "As the Systems Marshal is no doubt aware, most of our casualties in the conflict on Greaves have been due to Spasm darts."

The OB smiled. "The Marshal is also aware that those injuries not due to poison are, at best, suspect. There have been rumors of troopers shooting themselves in the feet, then claiming they were attacked by fifty of the Scum.

"Sir. If the Systems Marshal would examine the screen again—"

"Dammit, boy, I'm tired of playing games! What are you trying to avoid saying?"

The Lojt swallowed again. "Sir, the numbers."

Systems Marshal Venture, Over-Befalhavare for all of the Orm System, looked at the holoproj before him. What was the boy so scared shitless about? Khadaji's ammo consisted of 7612 rounds, from 10,000. Which meant he'd fired off, let's see, ten minus two is eight, nine minus one—

Venture stared at the screen as if it had suddenly told him to go fuck himself. It couldn't be. He checked his subtraction, but the numbers were right. Ten thousand darts. Take away those which had been recovered, seven thousand six hundred and twelve, and that meant the man had used twenty three hundred and eighty-eight. Venture's gaze travelled across the holoproj's split-screen to the number of poisoned Confederation troopers.

Two-three-eight-eight. The number was identical.

Venture looked up. "Are we certain of these figures, Lojt?"

"Yes sir. They've been checked and rechecked a dozen times."

"Holy Buddha's left nut," Venture said softly. "I can't believe it. The ratsucker was telling the truth! I will be *god*damned." The awe vanished, replaced by concern. "This can't get out, Lojtnant. I want to see some altered figures, stat. Some of those troopers were shot with other small arms, some wounded by explosions and what-not, do you understand? I want the changes in the computer within the hour."

"Sir."

"I also want arrests made, a few of the ringleaders of the Scum, let the records show, say, fifty were caught and executed, understand?"

"Understood, sir."

"One final thing. I want this *damped*. Anybody who came within a hundred meters of this information is to be cleaned thoroughly, this has got to be kept *quiet!* I don't want any of the troops to talk about it to *anybody,* I don't want *rumors,* I don't want the *slightest hint* of these numbers to get out. The Confed Military will be made to look like morons, including me *personally,* and anyone in my command who does that will regret it in ways you could not *begin* to believe, you copy?"

"Yes sir." The Lojt swallowed dryly.

But even as the young man executed a snappy about-face and marched from the office, Over-Befalhavare Venture knew it was probably too late. The soldiers' comline was faster than White radio; what one man or woman knew would be passed to another, despite attempts to prevent it. The story would out, eventually. They could deny it, of course, and PR would begin working on it ASAP, but it would be even worse if it smelled like a cover-up. Ah, damn! Why? What could have been on the man's mind, to take on an army, alone? And why give it up the way he did? The fucker must have been something else, too! *One dart per trooper. Never missed.* Buddha, wouldn't that stir the fucking underground! One goddamned man! He had to know it would get around, maybe even arranged it, maybe he had allies in the Military. Damn!

Pease cleared her throat politely, but Venture ignored her. After a moment, she spoke anyway. "It doesn't matter, sir, does it? I mean, the war on Greaves is over."

Blind and stupid, he thought. Aloud, he said, "Yes, the war on Greaves is over."

"And we won, sir."

It seemed to take him a long time to look away from the holoproj and up at the woman before the desk. Won? He laughed, and then spoke as if to a slow child. "No, Sub-

Befal Pease, *we* didn't win. All *we* did was kill him—that goddamned miserable elbow-sucker Khadaji *won!*"

And, of course, Over-Befalhavare Venture didn't know the half of it.

2.25

CYBERPUNK

___ **Islands in the Net** Bruce Sterling 0-441-37423-9/$4.50
Laura Webster is operating successfully in an age
where information is power--until she's plunged into a
netherworld of black-market pirates, new-age
mercenaries, high-tech voodoo...and murder.

___ **Neuromancer** William Gibson 0-441-56959-5/$4.99
The novel of the year! Case was the best interface
cowboy who ever ran in Earth's computer matrix. Then
he double-crossed the wrong people...

___ **Mirrorshades** Bruce Sterling, editor
0-441-53382-5/$4.99
The definitive cyberpunk short fiction collection,
including stories by William Gibson, Greg Bear, Pat
Cadigan, Rudy Rucker, Lewis Shiner, and more.

___ **Blood Music** Greg Bear 0-441-06797-2/$4.50
Vergil Ulam had an idea to stop human entropy—
"intelligent" cells—but they had a few ideas of their
own.

___ **Count Zero** William Gibson 0-441-11773-2/$4.50
Enter a world where daring keyboard cowboys break
into systems brain-first for mega-heists and brilliant
aristocrats need an army of high-tech mercs to make
a career move.